'I need to tell you something, Susie.'

'What?' She made no attempt to move, still standing by the door. He came over and took her hands in his, leading her over to a chair.

'Sit down.'

'I don't want to sit down,' she retorted.

'Can you feel that?' His voice was harsh, yet urgent. 'When I touch your hands? It's there, Susie. Whatever this thing is between us, it's there.'

'So? We don't have to act on it. You'll be gone at the end of the week and—'

'Susie.' He dropped her hands and took a few steps away. His actions were stiff and unnatural. Something was *really* wrong. 'We need to talk.'

'About what? About this attraction?'

'No. About my wife.'

Lucy Clark began writing romance in her early teens and immediately knew she'd found her 'calling' in life. After working as a secretary in a busy teaching hospital, she turned her hand to writing medical romance. She currently lives in South Australia with her husband and two children. Lucy largely credits her writing success to the support of her husband, family and friends.

You can visit Lucy's website at www.lucyclark.net or e-mail her at lucyclark@optusnet.com.au.

Recent titles by the same author:

THE FAMILY HE NEEDS
THE OUTBACK MATCH
EMERGENCY: DOCTOR IN NEED

THE VISITING SURGEON

BY
LUCY CLARK

MILLS & BOON®

To God—Without You, I am nothing.
James 5:15

First published in Great Britain 2002
Large Print edition 2003
Harlequin Mills & Boon Limited,
Eton House, 18-24 Paradise Road,
Richmond, Surrey TW9 1SR

© Lucy Clark 2002

ISBN 0 263 17977 X

Set in Times Roman 16½ on 17 pt.
17-0403-52292

Printed and bound in Great Britain
by Antony Rowe Ltd, Chippenham, Wiltshire

CHAPTER ONE

DR SUSIE MONAHAN brushed her hands apprehensively down her calf-length navy skirt and ensured her embroidered white blouse was tucked neatly into the waistband before shrugging into her matching navy jacket.

'Keep it cool.' She started to pace in front of her desk, taking deep breaths. 'Keep it cool.' She checked that none of her unruly auburn curls had managed to escape from the clip at the nape of her neck.

The buzz of the intercom on her desk startled her. She pressed the button. 'Yes, Todd?'

'The delegation is here.'

'Show them in, thank you.' She closed her eyes for a millisecond. How had she ever let herself be talked into this job? Acting Head of the orthopaedic department? It was ridiculous!

Not that she minded the administrative side but many other aspects of the job, such as lecturing and playing host to delegates, weren't her cup of tea. She was a doctor, not a tour guide!

Susie opened her eyes at the sound of the doorhandle being pulled down. Should she be sitting behind her desk? Should she be looking cool, calm and collected, as though she did this sort of thing every day? Too bad. She was standing like a statue in the middle of her own office with a fake smile pasted onto her face as a small group of people filed in.

The smile, however, became genuine when she found herself staring up at a man with the most gorgeous blue eyes she'd ever seen. He was tall—a lot taller than she'd expected. Probably about six feet four. His hair was a rich, dark brown and was fashionably short.

'I'm Jackson Myers,' he said, holding his hand out.

'Ah… Welcome.' She quickly recovered her composure. 'I'm Susan Monahan.' She placed her hand in his. His touch sent a jolt of electrifying tingles up her arm. His fingers gripped her hand firmly, warming not only her hand but the rest of her as well.

She'd been unprepared for such a reaction to this strange man. He held her hand for a fraction of a second longer than was necessary. His gaze locked with hers and Susie felt something wild pass between them—a connection. A flicker of surprise registered in his eyes before they both dropped their hands and took a small step backwards.

Whoa! What was that? He was a married man! Susie cleared her throat. 'Welcome... er...to Brisbane General Hospital, Professor Myers.'

'Please, call me Jackson.'

She rested a hand momentarily on her chest. 'I'm Susie.'

'Good. Well, then...Susie. Allow me to introduce you to the rest of my staff.' Jackson turned and introduced the people who were responsible for helping him keep to the strict timetable he lived by. As the visiting orthopaedic professor, Jackson had been touring the world for the past year and had now returned to his homeland of Australia. He had two secretaries, one research assistant, one technical consultant and a personal aide.

Susie's own secretary, Todd, was hovering by the door. She beckoned him in and introduced him. 'Todd and I are both at your service this week. If there's anything you need to know or can't find, please, don't hesitate to ask.' Susie addressed the group as she spoke but her gaze kept being drawn back to Jackson.

'Thank you,' he responded, their gazes holding again. Susie gave herself a mental shake and checked her watch.

'Right. I guess we should be making a start. Have there been any changes to the agreed agenda?'

'Not that I'm aware of. Richard?' Jackson turned and raised an inquisitive eyebrow at his personal aide. Richard shook his head.

'Good.' Susie nodded. 'Well, then, we'd better get started to ensure we don't fall behind schedule.' She smiled at Jackson and headed for the door. She waited for everyone else to go through. 'After you,' she said when only Jackson remained.

'Ladies first,' he insisted. He smiled at her and Susie felt her insides turn to mush. She was knocked off guard by the feeling but as she was unsure what to do about it she went through the door, mumbling, 'Thank you.' They headed out of the orthopaedic department towards the operating theatres, Susie pointing out different areas of the hospital as they went.

Once in Theatres, they did a tour of the operating room Jackson would be using when he taught. It had a viewing gallery positioned on a mezzanine floor surrounding the operating table so that students, interns and other surgeons could see what was happening with ease.

'It's also equipped with microphones and miniature cameras. The images can then be projected up onto the screen...' Susie pointed up to where a screen was fixed to the wall facing the gallery '...as well as being video-taped.'

'An impressive facility,' Jackson murmured. They continued with their tour, heading down yet another long corridor. 'This is the one characteristic all hospitals have—long corridors.'

Susie smiled up at him, pleasantly surprised to find he had a sense of humour and wasn't averse to sharing it with strangers. When she'd been planning for the visiting orthopaedic professor's visit, she hadn't given a lot of thought as to what type of man he might be. She'd just expected him to be a professional, which Jackson Myers was showing every indication of being. It was her *own* reaction that puzzled her more. She hadn't expected to be instantly attracted to a married man.

'All right, can everyone fit in the lift?' Susie asked as she held the doors open. 'Everyone in?' When she received affirmative murmurs, she allowed the doors to close and pressed the button for the fifth floor. 'The hospital's main lecture facility, which is where you'll be giving most of your lectures, had a complete upgrade last year. It's quite a nice facility to speak at,' she informed them. 'I've been assured that all the gadgets are in working order but if you find we don't have everything you require, please, let me know.'

'Thank you,' Jackson replied. When the lift doors opened, they all exited, again Jackson waiting until Susie had preceded him. She politely smiled her thanks, before leading the way to the lecture room. She pushed open the large double doors and watched as his team fanned out and checked out the facilities. It was quite funny to see them scuttling here and there, reporting back to each other and pointing things out.

Jackson walked over to the podium where Richard gave him several instructions as well as handing him a folder with notes inside. He familiarised himself with where his water glass would be, where to find the laser pointer and how to adjust the lapel microphone.

Susie wandered over to a seat in the front row and sat down, mesmerised by him. Lecturing wasn't one of her strong suits so she was always willing to learn. Just by watching him, she knew she could learn much.

Was that the real reason she was watching him? She tilted her head to the side, her gaze following his every move. He was very handsome. 'Pleasing to the eye', as her mother would have said. 'Hot to trot', would have been her oldest sister's opinion and 'big on the yum factor' youngest sister's contribution.

Susie found Jackson Myers…intriguing, and therefore a man to be avoided at all costs. After all, she was still recovering from a broken heart—her *second* broken heart, she corrected herself—and she didn't need a third. Two broken engagements were enough and Susie wasn't about to risk any involvement with the opposite sex, especially a liaison with a married man.

Then again, what did it matter if she enjoyed watching him? He'd be gone at the end of the week, off on the rest of his tour, and she could go back to her life. Surely there wasn't any harm in looking.

Someone sat in the chair next to her, bringing her out of her reverie. Was it time for people to start arriving already? She glanced up to find herself face to face with Jackson.

'Lost in thought?' His deep voice washed over her.

Susie laughed nervously. If only he *knew* where her thoughts had been. 'Bad habit,' she admitted.

'You were right. This is a great lecture room. One of the better ones.'

'I'm glad.' She checked her watch. 'Well, everyone should be starting to arrive soon.'

Jackson nodded but didn't move.

'You certainly have well-trained staff,' Susie commented, feeling the need to say something. His close proximity made her very self-conscious and some of her earlier apprehensiveness began to reappear.

'They are certainly that. At first it was all rather strange, having people bossing me about every step of the way, but now, after ten months of travelling and lecturing, I've learned to trust them. They're all extremely good at their jobs and if we each do our own thing and avoid getting in each other's way, things run smoothly.'

'I guess that's the name of the game when you're on one of these visiting professorships.'

'Absolutely.' A few people started to trickle in but still Jackson didn't move. He seemed quite settled where he was.

Susie fidgeted with her watch. 'Have you enjoyed it so far?'

'Yes,' he replied without hesitation. More people came in and started taking their seats. Jackson leaned a little closer to Susie, his elbow touching hers on the arm rest. She felt the warmth of him immediately, her breath catching in her throat as she waited for him to speak. 'Although, after ten months, I'm heartily sick of living out of a suitcase and waking up in a different city almost every day. Sometimes even a different country. Lots of flying. Only six weeks to go.' He turned his head as he spoke the last few words and looked at her. Their heads were almost touching and Susie found herself hypnotised by him. The tang of his aftershave teased at her senses and his breath slightly fanned her cheek. What was it about this man—this stranger—that drew her in?

'Jackson?' Richard called, and instantly the man beside her stood up and walked over to the podium. 'We'll just go over things one last time,' she heard Richard say, and continued to watch as Jackson patiently listened, nodding here and there to what he was being told.

Susie broke her gaze free of the enigmatic man. Don't focus on him, she told herself sternly. He's *male* and will no doubt break your heart—just like the others. Satisfied that she was now back in control of her emotions, Susie glanced around the room. When had it filled up? Almost every seat was taken and Richard now came over and sat down in the one next to her.

'Now, Susie, I believe you're introducing Jackson.' Richard shuffled through a few files, eventually finding the piece of paper he was looking for which confirmed the details.

Susie had completely forgotten. She'd been so caught up in…well…Jackson that she hadn't had time to think about standing up in front of such a large group of people. Todd sat down in the chair on her other side and handed her a folder.

'Here you go, boss. Knock 'em dead.' He patted her shoulder.

'What? Now?' she asked as Jackson came to sit on the other side of Richard.

'Now would be the perfect time,' Richard answered with an energetic nod.

She cleared her throat, 'Right, then.' As she stood, she smoothed down her skirt with her free hand and carried the folder to the podium. People stopped talking and the volume of noise in the room dropped rapidly. Susie opened the folder and took out the notes she'd prepared. Thank goodness Todd had brought them. She could always rely on Todd when it came to work.

Susie swallowed her nervousness, pushing it aside the way she usually did when she had to stand before a crowd. Giving her head a little flick, she straightened her shoulders and opened her mouth to speak.

'Thank you all for coming,' she said, mentally blocking out the sound of her own voice. 'We're gathered here today to welcome Professor Jackson Myers, the visiting orthopaedic professor, to Brisbane General Hospital.' She continued with the spiel about his accomplishments, his credits as a surgeon and mentioned some of the places he'd visited during the past ten months.

Soon she was inviting him to join her at the podium, which he did. He smiled politely and shook her hand, but this time she felt nothing but a cool reserve exuding from him. What had happened? Susie took her seat and watched him. Perhaps this was the 'public' side of him.

As he spoke, she pushed everything from her mind, listening to his deep, melodious tones. He had a wonderful speaking voice, one she could have listened to all day long. He didn't stutter, stumble or hesitate. Susie frowned, instantly cross with herself for studying the man instead of listening to what he was saying. She focused her thoughts and did just that.

Two hours later, when he finished, she was surprised at how quickly the time had passed. He was given a hearty round of applause which he accepted graciously before answering questions. After a further half-hour, people started to pour out of the lecture room. Jackson stayed where he was, answering yet more questions from people who approached him.

'Once we leave here,' Richard told her after he'd gathered up Jackson's notes, 'we'll be heading across the road to a restaurant for lunch. Correct?'

'Yes.'

'Is there anything you need to do or get before we go?'

'Yes.'

'Then do it now. Jackson will be about another ten minutes at least and we'll meet you in your office,' Richard said with a final nod before heading back to one of the secretaries to have a word with her.

'That went well,' Todd remarked as he accompanied Susie back to the department.

'Yes.' What was wrong with her? Was she completely incapable of stringing more that two words together?

'I'll just go over your schedule for the rest of the day.' Without waiting for Susie to reply, Todd read from a sheet in front of him. 'Lunch is next, where you'll be officially welcoming him to the department. The tutorial operating session is after lunch, where he'll be assisted by Mr Petunia, and then the official hospital faculty welcome dinner where you'll be the MC for the evening.' Todd chuckled. 'And as the MC, you'll be giving the official dinner welcome. Talk about pomp and ceremony.'

'That's the way these visiting professorships are handled,' Susie told him. 'Jackson represents the best of the best. It's a prestigious honour.'

'But one you'll never want,' Todd added. 'I saw how uneasy you were when you stood up there. I know you prefer not to speak in public, Susie.'

'Was I that obvious?' Susie was horrified.

'No. You looked as cool as a cucumber. Don't forget, I've been working with you for nine months now and already know your strengths and weaknesses.'

Susie smiled at the man who was the same age as her youngest brother. 'Todd, you have helped me out so much this year. I wouldn't have enjoyed this acting head stuff nearly as much otherwise.'

'Shucks,' he said as they walked into the department. 'You say the sweetest things.'

Susie laughed, glad to have the momentary respite from Jackson and his team. 'Let's get the rest of this day over and done with. Oh, and would you mind bringing me Jackson's dossier again? I just want to review some facts about him,' she added.

Todd brought the file through and left her alone. With trembling fingers, she flicked through the pages until she found the one she needed. Holding her breath, she scanned it quickly, hoping she'd previously read it wrong. Next to 'Marital Status' was the word 'Married'.

Lunch was a lavish affair for a 'few' special guests—all fifty of them. Susie accepted her notes from Todd, who was sitting opposite her, just before she was due to get up and talk. Having Jackson seated next to her didn't do anything to help her nerves.

When they'd arrived, he'd held her chair for her to be seated and Susie had politely thanked him. Was he just being nice? Did he want something? With it having been only six months since Greg had broken their engagement, Susie was very cautious of men and their motives.

She was extremely conscious of the warmth of his body so close to hers. His spicy aftershave smelt incredible and she did her best to fight the sensation it evoked. She didn't want to be so aware of him, yet she was.

She focused on the conversation taking place about the latest medical breakthrough, listening intently to Jackson's opinion on the subject. During their entrée and main course, Jackson answered many questions. It was a rare and unique opportunity to have access to someone who was travelling the world, hearing about and seeing at first hand new innovations in the ever-changing orthopaedic world, and her colleagues were making the most of it.

Just as their desserts were being brought around, Jackson stood and removed his suit jacket. Susie found her gaze drawn to his movements and she watched beneath her lashes, mesmerised by the way his triceps flexed beneath the material of his shirt. It almost made her hyperventilate. She took a sip from her water glass, breathing in as she swallowed.

Susie spluttered and started to cough. Jackson patted her on the back and everyone at their table stopped talking and watched her.

'You all right, Susie?' Jackson asked as he sat down again.

His concern was touching and she turned to look at him, an embarrassed smile on her face. She coughed again and nodded. 'I'm...' Another cough. 'Fine.' She didn't sound fine, even to her own ears, as the word had come out like a tiny squeak. Susie cleared her throat. 'Fine,' she reiterated more strongly.

Everyone resumed their conversations and she'd half expected Jackson to continue talking to Richard. Instead, he leaned over and refilled her water glass.

'Try it again.' He held the glass out to her and she took it. Their fingertips touched—just for an instant. It was enough to spread a deep warmth right throughout her body, causing her to gasp quietly. She was so aware of him it was ridiculous. Why couldn't she control herself?

Her smiled faded but she did as he'd suggested, conscious of the way he watched her actions. Their gazes held and Susie found herself powerless to look away. She rested the glass on her lower lip. As she tilted the liquid towards her mouth, she exhaled slowly, her breath steaming up the glass. She sipped and swallowed, replacing the glass on the table before her trembling fingers dropped it.

'There,' he whispered, but didn't smile. 'All better.' His gorgeous blue eyes were intense. Susie felt momentarily hypnotised. Within an instant, Jackson had somehow made her feel…desirable.

'Jackson will know.' Richard's voice intruded into the little bubble that surrounded them.

Jackson turned to face his right-hand man, a questioning look on his face. He tried desperately to listen to what Richard was asking, all the while trying to figure out what had just happened with Susie Monahan.

He'd been mesmerised by her. Had it been the way her lips had trembled ever so slightly as she'd rested the glass on her lips? Or the way they'd parted to allow the liquid to pass through? He swallowed convulsively and pushed thoughts of her from his mind, even though he was conscious of her every move.

Richard was still talking and, although Jackson could see his lips moving, he was having great difficulty in concentrating. Thankfully, the last few words sank in and he was able to answer the question in an authoritative and controlled manner.

Susie rose to her feet and quietly excused herself. Jackson glanced at her, noticing the way she smoothed her skirt down over her thighs. It wasn't the first time she'd done it and he'd realised earlier it was a display of uneasiness. Not that he was objecting, for each time she did it, it drew attention to her gorgeous legs.

Why was she uneasy? Had she felt that unmistakable pull of attraction between them? It had happened a number of times since he'd met her just a few short hours ago. There was definitely something between them and it was pulling them in like the vortex of a cyclone.

A mouth-watering chocolate dessert was placed before him but he pushed it away, not interested. He'd had enough of food...for the moment. He continued his discussion with Richard and other members of his table, forcing thoughts of Susie from his mind. He was a forty-one-year-old professional yet he was acting more like a hormonal teenager.

Just as he thought he'd succeeded, Susie returned to the table. He *felt* rather than saw her every move. Why was he so conscious of this woman? Of when she sat down. Of how her perfume teased at his senses, making him feel…intrigued and interested to know her better. It was ludicrous. He'd *never* felt such an instant attraction to a woman before and the knowledge troubled him.

Jackson turned slightly in his chair to face her and found her in discussion with Todd. Her hair was the most stunning colour and he wondered for a moment whether it was natural. Jackson found himself growing impatient for her to finish speaking so *he* could have her attention. He shook his head slightly. What was wrong with him today?

Finally, Susie turned to look at him. 'Feeling better?' His tone was soft and intimate. How had *that* happened?

'Yes, thank you.' She was touched by his concern. 'It was, um, silly of me…to choke on my water like that. Then again,' she said with a small chuckle, 'I'm usually the person who drops their knife on the floor and that sort of thing.'

Jackson smiled at her confession. 'Were you clumsy as a child?'

Susie thought for a moment. 'Not that I can remember, but I'm sure my parents would have a different answer. My mother has the most amazing memory, and as I'm number four out of ten that's quite a memory.'

'Ten children?' Jackson was astounded. 'You have nine brothers and sisters?'

'Yes.' Susie was used to this sort of reaction and smiled. 'It was fantastic, growing up in a large family. The only downside is shopping for Christmas. All of those nieces and nephews!' She chuckled and Jackson joined in. 'How about you?' Even as she heard the words come out of her mouth, seemingly of their own volition, Susie found she couldn't stop herself. She *wanted* to know more about him. 'Any siblings?'

He nodded. 'I have younger twin sisters who even now can't resist sticking their noses into my life.'

'You can't keep anything from my family, either. Nothing at all,' Susie agreed. 'The only time I think we've successfully kept a secret was two years ago when we all banded together and gave my parents a surprise forty-fifth wedding anniversary party.'

'That would have been a party to remember.'

'It was.' Their gazes held again and she felt her smile begin to fade. That underlying tug of attraction was starting to wind its way around them and she desperately fought for something to say that would break the moment. 'You haven't touched your dessert. Don't you have a sweet tooth?'

'Not really. I used to before I started this tour but I've had so many working dinners and lunches—even breakfasts—that my sweet tooth has definitely disappeared.'

'That's a lot of food.'

'Absolutely.' He smiled. 'But it gives me the opportunity to speak to more people and that's one of the main aims of visiting professorships.'

'Excuse me, Susie,' Todd interrupted, 'I've just had a call from Mr Petunia's office.'

'Problem?'

'One of his private patients is having complications.'

'He's gone to Theatre,' Susie stated, and automatically checked her watch. Todd nodded.

'Something wrong?' Richard asked, his radar ears picking up the conversation.

'Mr Petunia, the surgeon who was scheduled to assist Jackson in Theatre this afternoon, has been called to an emergency.'

'He can't make it!' Richard's tone rose rapidly.

'Relax, Richard,' Jackson said as he watched his aide stand up and start pacing.

'I'm sure we can find someone else to assist,' Susie added quickly. 'The viewing gallery will be filled with orthopaedic surgeons who would give anything to work alongside the VOP.' She turned to find Jackson eyeing her carefully.

'Susie will do it,' he told Richard.

'Me?' Susie shook her head. The last thing she wanted was to be by his side in Theatre, with people watching her. 'But I'm an upper-limb specialist.'

'So? You're more than capable. I've read the dossier on Dr Susan Monahan, MBBS, FRACS, Ph.D, MD. It stated that your sub-speciality is upper limb with an interest in microsurgery. Admirable, I must say,' he added.

'Don't try and flatter me, Jackson.' She worked hard to control her rising anger at his blatant manipulation. She needed to be diplomatic. 'There are plenty of other orthopods who'd be more than willing to assist you.'

'That may be but I choose you. I'm sure you've already studied the procedure as you seem like the type of person who doesn't leave anything to chance.' He rubbed his hands together and stood before she could say another word. 'All fixed, then. Richard...'

Susie watched him as he talked with his aide. 'But I'm an upper-limb specialist,' she reiterated, her voice rising slightly.

Jackson merely smiled and nodded. She didn't want to cause a scene and as this was his first day here, she knew she was bound to do whatever she could to facilitate things. Damn politics! She hated them.

'You OK, Susie?' Todd asked as he sank down into the seat Jackson had just vacated. 'You're looking a little pale.'

'I *have* to assist him.' She said the words slowly and shook her head in annoyance.

'Wow. You're going great guns today. For someone who doesn't like being the centre of attention, you're certainly having your fair share of it.'

'I didn't *choose* to do it. I was *told* to do it,' she said between clenched teeth.

'Ah...politics.' Todd chuckled.

'I'm glad you find this so amusing,' she grumbled.

'Don't you feel confident?'

'About the actual surgery? Yes. Having everyone watch me? Not really, but I'm sure I'll get by.'

'I'll go now and make sure everyone who needs to know about the change does. It's almost time for Jackson to head back so I'll see you over there soon.'

She watched Todd as he stopped and spoke to both Jackson and Richard before continuing out the door. Richard followed him and soon Jackson was standing there by himself. Susie was about to get up and walk over to tell the VOP that she didn't like other people making decisions for her but he turned and walked out a side door.

Accepting her fate, Susie reached for her water glass again and drank the contents. That would be her last drink until she came out of Theatre, which would be around five-thirty that afternoon.

Jackson stood looking up at the blue sky that was littered with white fluffy clouds. He'd never been to Brisbane before and it looked as though this time all he'd be seeing would be the inside of lecture rooms and operating theatres. That was how it had been for most of his tour.

He'd seen and operated with some of the best surgeons in the world and now he'd asked Susie to assist him. He was in two minds at the moment. He was interested in seeing her skills, but from his experience of this morning his libido seemed to run away without his permission whenever she got within speaking distance of him.

It worried him a little. All right, it worried him a lot. Even with Alison, he'd never felt that strong pull of attraction—the unwanted attraction that made him so aware of every move Susie made. Sitting next to her at lunch had been…disastrous, as well as pleasurable.

Jackson closed his eyes, picturing Alison. Sweet, vivacious Alison who'd urged him to do this professorship in the first place. He missed her so much. Yet here he was, feeling an attraction to Susie that he seemed unable to stop.

What was he going to do?

CHAPTER TWO

'SUCTION,' Jackson ordered, and Susie complied. They'd been in Theatre for almost four hours now and Jackson looked as fresh as when he'd first walked in. At the beginning, Susie had been very conscious of the packed viewing gallery, but once the operation had begun she'd pushed it to the back of her mind. She had a job to do and she was going to do it.

They still had an hour left to go for this procedure, which was a pelvic reconstruction. Jackson's research in this field had led him to invent a device that made certain aspects of the surgery more manageable. He'd been extensively published in several of the world's leading orthopaedic journals, which was one of the reasons why he'd been chosen for this visiting professorship. And here she was, operating alongside him!

In some ways, she felt as though she should have refused him in order to let a lower-limb specialist assist, but the rarity of the opportunity had struck a chord with her. Besides, when Jackson had asked, she'd been immediately flattered. Flattered that he thought she was worth asking. His gaze had encompassed her so completely, as though the two of them had been the only ones in the room.

'Good,' he said. 'Now, we'll start reducing the posterior aspect of the fracture. I'll be fixing a one, eight-hole, three-and-a-half-millimetre reconstruction plate, securing it in place with two screws at either end.' Jackson spoke in his normal tone, knowing his words would be picked up on the microphone that was situated within the theatre.

When the viewing gallery had been built, the actual operating room had undergone a transformation as well. Small cameras had been installed, enabling everyone to see the procedure being performed. Apart from general teaching, this was the first time the theatre had been used for a visiting specialist.

'I'll need an interfragmentary screw as well to keep that acetabular margin firmly in place,' Jackson said once the reconstruction plate had been affixed. He'd already used two interfragmentary screws on the iliac crest during the anterior fixation of the pelvis.

As with all operations, it was necessary to have everything the surgeon might require sterilised and ready to go, rather than have the operation come to a standstill in the middle of the procedure. That would never do—especially with a visiting surgeon.

It had only happened to Susie once before, but as she'd been in a Third World country, where medical supplies and equipment had been scarce, it hadn't been such a big surprise.

'Swab.' A few moments later, Jackson glanced at Susie and she read the satisfaction in his gaze. The look made her feel as though they were sharing a special secret. 'I'm happy with that. Check X-ray, please.' While they waited for the radiographer to come and take the X-ray, Jackson looked up at the viewing gallery and explained some of the finer points of the surgery he'd just performed.

Susie allowed herself a brief glance up, only to see several heads in the gallery bowed as students, interns and registrars alike furiously took notes. Thanks to the cameras, though, it meant a permanent record would be kept of this procedure so anyone who had missed it could hire the video from the library.

Susie had never been more glad to walk out of Theatre and into the changing rooms. She sat down in a chair and let her arms hang limp by her side. Closing her eyes, she rested her head back and took a deep, relaxing breath.

Operating with Jackson had been a wonderful experience career-wise, but during the first few minutes of the procedure she'd been so acutely aware of him that her heart had been beating a wild tattoo against her ribs. Forcing her professionalism to the front, Susie had pretended he'd been just like anyone else she'd operated with. She'd been able to anticipate his needs, which had been another thing she'd been concerned about.

Although she hadn't been the centre of attention, Susie had still felt as though she'd been trapped like a mouse in a cage. All those people, watching everything they'd done. Relax, she told herself. It's over. Everything had gone fine. There had been no complications, no awkward moments. Jackson had been very explicit in what he'd wanted each member of theatre staff to do, and Susie realised he was used to operating with unfamiliar staff.

She opened her eyes and shook her head. No way in the world would she ever be able to cope with the pressures of a visiting professorship. She was a good surgeon, and that was enough for her. The opportunity to do further research into microsurgical techniques of the hand and fingers was definitely enough to keep her occupied for quite some time. She started to get changed and was just tucking in her shirt when a few of the nurses came in.

'Wow!' one of them said, fanning her face. 'He is one gorgeous man. Pity he's married.'

'No.' Another nurse shook her head emphatically. 'He's divorced, at least that's what I heard.'

Susie clenched her jaw and tried not to listen.

'Uh-uh,' a third nurse added. 'His wife died.'

'His dossier said he was married,' the first nurse reiterated. 'Have you heard anything, Susie?'

'About what?' Susie pulled the pins out of the bun in which she'd secured her hair for Theatre and started to brush it out. She hated gossip.

'About Professor Myers!' the nurse exclaimed. 'Honestly, Susie. You should get out from behind that desk or operating table or whatever it is you hide behind more often because that man is so hot.'

Susie clipped her hair back in its usual style and looked at them. 'He's certainly a great surgeon,' she replied, and the nurses groaned. There was no way she was going to tell them that he set her blood pumping, made her knees go weak and took her breath away all with one smouldering, sexy look!

'Is that all you can see?'

'What's wrong with admiring a man for his brains and his skill, as well as his looks?'

'So you think he *is* good-looking?'

'I didn't dispute the fact,' she pointed out as she closed her locker. 'Right now, though, I need to go home and change before this evening's event.'

'Lucky thing. You get to sit next to him and everything,' one of the nurses complained. 'While we'll be at the back of the room...'

'Admiring him from afar,' another one finished. They sighed in unison.

'See you tonight, ladies.' Susie walked out of the room and headed back to her office. She needed to check her in-tray and make sure everything was up to date. She opened her office door and jumped in fright when she saw Jackson sitting next to her desk.

'Jackson! What are...? I thought you'd gone.' Her stomach lurched in delight. She told herself off and forced her legs to work, walking over to her desk where she quickly sat down.

'I wanted to thank you for assisting me.'

She smiled. 'It should be I who's thanking you for the opportunity. Or should I thank Mr Petunia's emergency?'

Jackson chuckled. 'Either way, it was great to be able to work with you.'

'You made everything easy for me…and the rest of the staff,' she added. She looked at him for a second, tilting her head to the side. 'Are you always so…direct in Theatre or is it just because you have an audience?'

He nodded. 'The audience, although I've become accustomed to having people watch me.'

'Well, you're certainly very good at what you do. You almost make me want to change my sub-speciality.' She idly shifted some paper around before placing her hands palms down on the desk in an effort to control her wayward emotions.

'Really? Now, that would be an accomplishment worth noting on my résumé.' He smiled at her and Susie felt all warm and gooey inside.

'Almost,' she pointed out. Her intercom buzzed and she pressed the button. 'Yes, Todd?'

'I'm going now, Susie. Was there anything else you needed?'

She glanced around her desk, checking her in-tray. There were three pieces of paper in there. 'Do I need to do these things in my in-tray now?'

'Not urgent,' he told her. 'Do them after ward round tomorrow.'

'All right. See you tonight, Todd.'

'Yeah, but only if I can tie that bow-tie thing straight. Who made it a formal dinner, eh?'

'We can blame Richard,' Jackson called loudly, and Todd chuckled before saying good-bye. 'He's good,' Jackson said. 'How long has he been working with you?'

'No.' Susie shook her head. 'The question you should be asking is how long have I been working with *him*? He's been the secretary to the head of orthopaedics for the past three years. I only started nine months ago.'

'How old is he? He looks about seventeen.'

'Shh.' Susie giggled. 'Don't tell him that. He's still trying to fight his cute baby-face looks. He's twenty-four and an excellent sec-retary.' Susie pulled her bag out of a drawer before locking her desk. 'When the head of de-partment was taken ill at the beginning of this year, it was Todd who helped me find my feet. Without him, I'd have gone down the gurgler ages ago.'

'So you're not into hospital politics? Administration?'

'Not really.' Susie stood and motioned to the door. 'We'd better make a move or I'll end up being late for dinner.'

'Sure.' Jackson followed her out of her office and waited while she locked it. Susie turned and bumped into him. She hadn't realised he'd been standing so close.

'Sorry,' she mumbled, and quickly took a step to the side. She glanced down at the floor, trying desperately to control the mass of tingles that were now raging rampantly throughout her body. Susie kept her head down as she moved a few steps away before raising her head to look at him. One of her curls had managed to escape from its bonds and swung down beside her cheek.

With a feather-light touch, Jackson reached out and gently tucked it behind her ear. The feel of his skin against hers caused her to catch her breath as she gazed up at him. Further down the corridor, a door closed with a thud and Susie jumped in fright.

'Ah... Are you...? I mean...do you...um?' She stopped and forced herself to take a steadying breath. 'How are you getting back to the hotel? Do you need a lift?'

Jackson nodded, a slow smile forming on his lips. 'That would be great. Thanks.'

'Car park is this way.' Without waiting for further communication from him, Susie headed off down the corridor and turned right at the end. She opened a door and started heading down the stairs. She was acutely aware of Jackson following her and it wasn't until they'd gone down three flights of stairs that she pushed open the door that led to the street.

'I'm parked over here,' she told him as they walked side by side.

'So, the previous head of ortho. You said he was taken ill?'

'Yes, in February. Myocarditis. He was working out this year and had planned to retire at the end of it. Now he's retired early.'

'So he's not coming back?'

'No. He's officially resigned from the hospital.'

'Which leaves you in charge?'

'Well, they have to advertise the position. I'm only Acting Head until the end of this year,' she told him as she stopped by her white Jaguar Mark-II. She unlocked the door. 'So, when you finish your tour, do you want a job?' she chuckled.

'This is *your* car?' Jackson frowned in disbelief.

'Yes. Why? You sound surprised.' Susie climbed in and reached over to unlock the passenger door.

'Sorry.'

'Aren't women allowed to drive sports cars?' she teased with a smile. The smile soon disappeared as she surreptitiously watched him sink down into the seat. The way the fabric of his trousers was pulled taut over his quadriceps made her breathing increase. He had a good body. No denying that. She quickly turned in case he should see her gawking at him, and concentrated on putting on her seat belt.

'Of course not,' he replied.

'Do you like Jaguars?' Why did her voice sound so husky? She cleared her throat and put the key into the ignition before starting the engine.

'I drive the Mark-V. Well, when I'm in Melbourne,' he clarified.

'And not jet-setting around the world, showing off your brilliance,' Susie couldn't resist teasing lightly. Oh, my gosh, she thought. I'm flirting with him! Jackson laughed and the sound washed over her with joy. She had made him laugh.

'So how long have you been a Jaguar fan?' he asked as she navigated her way out of the car park.

'For as long as I can remember. My father and brothers have always had a passion for them. They restored this one for mc.'

'Wow. That's something I've always wanted to get into. Restoring vintage cars.'

'It can get very messy. I've lost count of the number of times my mother said she'd throw things away if they didn't clean up. In the end, my dad built a huge shed in the back paddock of the property they live on, and every night the ''junk'', as my mother affectionately calls it, is locked up out of her sight.'

'Your entire face lights up when you speak about your family.' Jackson's tone was soft and intimate, making Susie extremely conscious of the small space they were in. 'It's great that you have such a loving relationship with them,' he continued a few seconds later.

'We're a close lot.' She paused for a moment before saying, 'You sound close to your sisters.'

He laughed. 'Yes.'

'Do they live near you?'

'Cindy's in Melbourne, but Candy's in New Zealand. Since my father died, my mother spends her time alternating between the two of them. Six months in NZ and six months here. Well, in Melbourne,' he clarified again.

'Of course.' Susie smiled. She stopped at a red light and turned to look at him, only to find him studying her. To her surprise, he didn't look away.

Slowly, he reached out and tucked the same stray curl behind her ear. 'You're a very beautiful woman, Susie.' The deep resonance of his voice washed over her. Her heart doubled its rhythm and she felt her hands begin to perspire.

He's married, he's married, he's married, she chanted to herself.

Jackson's fingers gently caressed her cheek, lightly touched her lips. Susie breathed out heavily, unable to believe the mounting tension spiralling within her. Abruptly, he broke the contact, his arm jerking back to his side as though burnt. He looked away. 'Light's green.'

'Wh—? Oh.' Susie frowned in confusion before returning her attention to the road. The atmosphere in the car was now one of strained silence. What should she do now? Should she ask him why he thought she was beautiful? No. That would look as though she was fishing for a compliment. Oh, she was no good at this. She was no good in romantic situations.

Jackson cleared his throat. 'I gather you won't be applying for the job you're doing now?'

Susie tried to focus her thoughts. 'Probably not.'

'You really don't like the administration, do you?'

'Not particularly. How about you?'

'It doesn't bother me. Especially after this year.'

'I guess you don't have much time to relax.'

'Not really. Depending on where we are or what we're doing, I sometimes get a bit of free time, but nine times out of ten Richard will plan something else.' Jackson shrugged, as though he didn't really care one way or the other.

Susie didn't envy him at all. In fact, she felt quite sorry for him *and* his wife. It was no way to conduct a marriage as far as she was concerned. No way could she stand for her husband to be away for twelve months with only the odd phone call here and there. For a moment she wasn't sure what to say and the silence began to stretch. Say something, she told herself. Anything to break the awkwardness that was enveloping both of them. 'So I guess the VOP definitely cuts into your family time.'

He glanced at her and frowned. Oops. Had she overstepped the mark? She was just about to apologise for her statement when he said, 'It's not too bad. I managed to see Candy when I was in New Zealand so that was a bonus.'

It was Susie's turn to frown as she pulled into the entrance of the hotel. Why was he talking about his sisters? She'd meant the family life he shared with his wife. A valet attendant opened the passenger door for Jackson, thereby ending all conversation.

'Thanks for the lift.' He looked into her eyes and smiled politely. 'See you in a few hours.'

'See you then,' she replied, just as politely.

They were strangers, Susie reminded herself as she drove towards her house. What had she expected? He thought she was beautiful—so what? Why couldn't a man tell a woman she was beautiful and leave it at that? Probably because, apart from family members who didn't really count, very few men had said those words to her.

She'd been the little girl with red hair and freckles when she'd been younger. Her mother had always raved about the colour of her hair, calling Susie her auburn beauty. As she'd grown older her hair had darkened but, when placed amongst raven-haired sisters, Susie had often felt inadequate. Not that they'd ever made her feel that way—quite the opposite.

Susie pulled into her driveway and garaged her car. She sat there for a few minutes, thinking about Jackson Myers. He was a nice, charming man. Gorgeous and intelligent. And he was leaving at the end of the week!

Jackson scanned the crowded outer room which was starting to fill up. The dinner this evening was in his honour, as were most of the dinners he attended. When he'd first started on the VOP tour, he'd been astounded at the number of dinners he would have to attend. Now, though, he was becoming an expert at them.

At least in his medical lecturing he'd been able to write new lectures. Sharing and passing on information he'd learnt during his tour. He was thankful for the variety it offered.

His gaze scanned the room as people started making their way through to the ballroom whilst others were just arriving. He checked his watch. Five minutes late already. Richard would be having a fit. Where was Susie? They couldn't start without her. She was the MC.

He looked around again and realised he'd been unconsciously searching for her from the moment he'd walked in. Someone came up, introduced themselves and shook hands with him. Jackson listened to the questions being asked of him and gave the usual replies, allowing his gaze to flick to the door every few seconds.

'Excuse me,' Richard said. 'It's time to begin.'

Jackson shook hands with the person he'd been speaking to and allowed Richard to lead him away. 'Susie's not here yet,' Jackson pointed out.

'If we wait any longer, we'll be getting to bed after midnight.'

'We'll be getting to bed after midnight, anyway. We'll wait for her,' he told Richard firmly. His aide gave him a look that said he wasn't happy with the situation but acquiesced. Most of the time, Jackson considered himself a reasonable man and usually allowed himself to be 'looked after' by his staff. After all, if one event ran over time they were out for the rest of the day, but at this time of the evening it really made no difference whether they started early, late or on time.

He checked his watch again. Ten minutes late. He started to worry, hoping nothing bad had happened. Jackson shook his head. Alison had been three hours late and he'd been telling himself *then* not to worry, and all the time she'd been... He stopped his train of thought. This was no time to be thinking about Alison.

Todd came through the doors and Jackson almost pounced on him. 'Do you know where Susie is?'

'She's not here yet?' Todd asked in surprise.

'No.'

'OK,' he said, and pulled out his mobile phone. A few seconds later he left a message on her voicemail. 'Phone's off. She could be at the hospital.'

'Of course,' Jackson replied, starting to relax again. He waited anxiously while Todd rang the orthopaedic ward and spoke to someone there. He nodded to Jackson. 'She's just left?' Todd said into the receiver. 'Good. Thanks.' He disconnected the call. 'She left the hospital a few minutes ago. She shouldn't be long now.'

'I hope everything's all right.'

'Knowing Susie, it will all be under control. She's a great doctor.' Todd shook his head mockingly. 'Not so great a head of department, but a great doctor.'

'I guess that's what's important.' Jackson smiled, feeling more relaxed. 'Why don't you go on in and tell Richard what's happening?' he suggested. 'I'll wait for her.'

'You just don't want to face Richard,' Todd said with a knowing nod, and Jackson laughed.

'Caught me out.' As he watched Todd go, he knew facing Richard wasn't the reason he didn't want to go in. He wanted to see Susie with his own eyes. To make sure she was OK. There were still other people trickling in so she wasn't all *that* late, even though his aide would disagree. Jackson walked over to the wall and looked unseeingly at a painting. Why? Why was he so concerned about her? He'd been astounded at his reaction to her when she'd driven him to the hotel.

He'd wanted to kiss her!

The knowledge had shocked him and he'd told himself sternly that it was just a physical attraction. Nothing more. Besides, he was leaving at the end of the week, with six more weeks left of the tour. Nothing could happen between him and Susie, even if he wanted it to. And then there was Alison.

'Jackson?'

At the sound of Susie's voice, he spun on his heel and gazed at her.

'What are you doing out here? I thought we were supposed to have started by now.'

Jackson felt as though he'd just been slugged in the solar plexus. She looked…stunning.

Dressed in an off-the-shoulder, black-beaded dress that shimmered when she walked, Susie was a vision of loveliness. The dress was expertly cut, falling to mid-calf and moulded superbly to her shape. Her auburn tresses had been wound on top of her head with a few loose tendrils springing down. She wore a necklace with a small square-cut diamond pendant attached and matching diamond studs in her ears.

'I wanted to wait for you.' His tone was thick with desire. 'I'm glad I did. You look…beautiful…breathtaking.'

At his words, Susie floated up to the clouds. His words held sincerity and the way he was looking at her backed them up. Jackson *really* thought she looked breathtaking. She took a small step closer, her gaze never leaving his. 'Thank you, Jackson. That's the nicest thing a man has said to me in a long time.'

She was still trying to come to terms with how incredible he looked in his tuxedo. When she'd walked in her knees had almost given way. As she was wearing three-inch heels, the result would have been disastrous. Thankfully, she'd been able to hold onto a vestige of control.

He gazed at her, wondering whether it would be inappropriate to devour the MC by smothering her with kisses. Instead, he indicated the ballroom. 'Shall we?'

They crossed the floor and entered the ballroom which had been set up according to her seating plan. Several people were still finding their seats and as Jackson and Susie worked their way towards their table, they were stopped by people wanting to meet the famous Professor Myers.

As they continued to move towards their seats, Susie walked ahead of him. It was then that Jackson realised her dress had a split at the back, revealing a generous amount of her leg— her shapely calves, the indent of her knees and a brief glimpse of her thighs.

He swallowed and ran a finger around the collar of his shirt, forcing himself to look away. He concentrated on the carpet, but once they reached their table he held her chair while she sat, sneaking one last glance at her sexy legs.

Ten minutes later, she was standing to give her welcome speech while Jackson forced himself not to lean back in his chair to sneak another glance at her legs.

Susie was very conscious of Jackson sitting beside her, the warmth radiating from him making her feel parched. She forced herself, however, to continue but was grateful to hand over to Jackson and sit down again.

Jackson stood and spoke with ease to the two hundred or so people gathered in groups at their round tables. His deep, melodious tone washed over her and Susie admired the way he threw in little anecdotes, working his way through what he wanted to say without the prompting of notes in front of him. Then again, she remembered he'd had a lot of experience standing up in front of people.

'You didn't do too badly,' Todd said later as he crouched by her chair. She was completely surrounded by males as she was the only female seated at her table. Although the dinner had been open to consultants and their partners, many had come by themselves. As Susie was currently the only female orthopaedic surgeon in Brisbane, she was used to feeling a little outnumbered!

'I could say the same thing for your bow-tie. How long did it take you to do that?' she asked as she adjusted it.

'Ages. I only arrived a few minutes before you and I didn't even have the excuse of having to stop by the hospital.'

Susie raised her eyebrows. 'Checking up on me?'

'Jackson was concerned,' Todd told her with a shrug, and stood. 'I'll catch up with you later. There are a few nurses I want to impress while I'm dressed up like this.'

Susie chuckled as he headed off but his final words stayed with her. Jackson had been concerned about her? She risked a glance at him as he spoke to someone across the table. Had he *really* been worried about her or the dinner starting on time?

Susie's head was starting to spin. She needed some space. She picked up her clutch evening bag and rose. 'Excuse me,' she said softly. Every man at the table stood politely as she left.

As Susie walked away from the table, Jackson found his gaze drawn to the sway of her hips and her gorgeous legs. Once more he forced himself to look away, returning his attention to Richard, only to realise his aide was watching Susie as well.

In fact, all the men at the table were watching her. 'Wow!' one of them remarked. 'Susie looks…'

'Like a woman,' one of the other men finished, and they all laughed.

Jackson felt his hackles begin to rise. 'Problem?'

'This is the first time Susie's worn a dress to an official departmental function,' someone told him. 'So it's the first opportunity we've had to see her in anything other than a suit.'

'She sure looks different. If being Head of Department means Susie wears a dress like that, she has my support for the job.'

'She's also a colleague of yours,' Jackson pointed out. 'Please, show her the respect she deserves.' He knew his tone sounded pompous and arrogant but he couldn't help himself. He wasn't at all happy that other men were ogling the woman *he* found desirable. 'You were saying, Richard?' Jackson turned his attention to his aide.

He still found it hard to concentrate on what Richard was saying, his thoughts caught up with Susie and how incredible she looked in that dress. Especially when she walked. He was unable to control his thoughts, growing more impatient for her return with every passing second. Was she all right? Had anything happened to upset her?

A few minutes later his gaze strayed to the doorway again and this time he almost breathed a sigh of relief as he watched her return. Her hips swished slightly and he noticed she was concentrating hard on balancing in her shoes. She looked...gorgeous. Unlike the other men at the table, he hadn't needed to see her in that sexy black dress to realise she was all woman beneath it. He'd realised that fact the first moment he'd laid eyes on her that morning.

He excused himself from what Richard was saying and held out Susie's chair as she sat.

'Thank you,' she said, and smiled at him. He really was quite the gentleman. He included her in the conversation he was having with Richard, but not ten minutes later her mobile phone rang.

'Excuse me,' she said as she fished it out of her bag. Jackson was aware of her quiet tone as she spoke. Moments later, she ended the call.

'It looks as though I'll have to pass on coffee,' she told everyone at the table.

'Emergency?' Jackson asked.

'Yes.' At the interested glances she received, she elaborated. 'Fractured olecranon, radius and ulna. My registrar says he's showing signs of compartment syndrome.'

'What's that?' Richard asked, and several of the surgeons seated at their table started to answer.

'It's Susie's patient,' Jackson intervened. 'I think she's more than capable of answering Richard's question.'

Susie turned slightly to look at Richard. 'It's the effect of tissue swelling within a compartment of the body, in this case the forearm. The blood vessels are being compressed, which results in muscle atrophy.'

'So…that's kind of bad,' Richard reasoned.

'Yes.' She smiled at him.

'Can't your registrar deal with it?' Richard asked. 'You are the MC after all.'

'Sorry, but it's a private patient,' Susie explained as she picked up her bag.

'I think she's fulfilled her MC duties for the evening,' Jackson told his aide.

When she stood, all the men rose to their feet. 'Oh, please, sit down,' she said with a smile, before turning to Jackson. 'Sorry to run out on your welcome dinner but these things can't be helped.'

Jackson remained standing. 'No need to apologise. Besides, we're almost done.' They shook hands and again Susie felt that warm buzz of excitement spread up her arm. She nodded politely before dropping his hand and walking away from the table. She was stopped a few times on her way out, but as the room was filled with people linked to the medical profession they all understood the demands of emergencies.

As she took the lift down to the ground floor, waiting with mild impatience while the valet collected her car, Susie fought for self-control. In less than twenty-four hours she'd met a man who affected her like no one else ever had, and she was having difficulty getting him out of her mind.

Be careful, she told herself sternly. You've been burnt twice already. First by Walter and then by Greg. It will do you no good to get involved with the handsome Jackson Myers, despite his charm. That would just be asking for trouble.

She drove carefully to the hospital, heading straight for the emergency theatres. She changed into theatre clothes and went in search of her registrar.

'Nice hairdo,' Kyle, her registrar, teased and she laughed.

'How's Mr Barnes?'

'Coping well. I've explained what's happening to him and he's signed the consent form. The instruments and Theatre are ready. We're just waiting on the all-clear from the anaesthetist.'

'Excellent.' Susie went to see her patient and have a word with the anaesthetist before checking the notes Kyle had taken during the evening. When everything was organised, they started to scrub.

Once in Theatre, Susie had her mind in gear and off Jackson Myers. She focused her attention on Mr Barnes's arm, which he'd injured whilst playing tennis.

'Why do people persist in playing sport?' Susie asked her registrar as they relieved the pressure of the tissue planes. 'They only end up injuring themselves.'

'They keep fit. They enjoy themselves. They meet new people.'

'I can do all that without playing sport,' she told him, smiling beneath her mask. 'There are just some games I don't understand. I mean, why would a person play something like…beach volleyball, for instance? First of all, they usually don't wear shoes, which heightens circumstances for stress fractures. They're jumping all around, up and down on the sand, landing on their ribs as well as arms and legs. A whole list of orthopaedic injuries spring to mind, and all for what? So they can enjoy themselves? Rent a movie—it's safer!'

Kyle laughed. 'How many beach volleyball games have you seen?'

'None,' she replied. 'But I've seen the injuries. I'm sure it's not *totally* bad. There are plenty of worse sports.'

'Like motorcycle racing?' Kyle asked, knowing full well this was one of Susie's pet hates.

'Don't get me started. I've been in a pretty good mood today, considering.'

'Yes, you have,' he approved. 'Glad the VOP is finally under way?'

'Most definitely. One day down, five more to go.' Kyle had known she hadn't wanted to act as host for the VOP and had tolerated her mounting apprehensiveness with a cool, calm and collected attitude.

'I take it the dinner went well.'

'Yes.' Susie frowned.

'The VOP seems like a nice guy.'

'Did you manage to get to the viewing gallery this afternoon?'

'I came in late. Couldn't see much. You, on the other hand, certainly had a bird's-eye view. How did that happen?'

Susie growled and told him about Mr Petunia's cancellation while she inserted a drain into Mr Barnes's arm, which would hopefully ensure against further recurrence of compartment syndrome. 'So Jackson *told* me I was the replacement.'

'What was it like? I mean, operating with one of the greats.'

She heard the door to her theatre open but thought nothing of it. 'What was it like? It was scary, that's what it was like.' Susie paused for a moment. 'Not scary *assisting* Jackson, no, that was fine, but having all those people watching? No, thank you.'

'Jackson, eh?' Kyle teased. 'On a first-name basis with him already?'

'What do you expect me to call him? Professor? His Excellency? Brilliant Surgeon?' The most sexiest man alive? she thought. She heard someone slowly walk around the table and come to stand behind Kyle.

Susie frowned and raised her gaze to look past Kyle's shoulder. Her eyes widened in surprise as she looked directly into Jackson's deep blue ones.

CHAPTER THREE

'I'D SETTLE for the last one,' Jackson said in that deep tone she was becoming accustomed to.

Susie quickly put a dampener on the frisson of awareness his close proximity caused. For a second she thought she'd spoken her last one out loud and lowered her gaze, forcing herself to concentrate on her work. She was almost ready to close.

'Jackson,' she said, hoping her voice didn't betray the surprise, elation and confusion she felt at his unannounced presence. 'What brings you here?'

'Curiosity.'

'For compartment syndrome?'

He chuckled, and Susie locked the sound away in her memory, promising herself to re-live it later.

'Introduce us,' Kyle whispered, and Susie cleared her throat.

'Jackson, this is my registrar, Dr Kyle Thompson, who is going to help me to close up Mr Barnes's arm so we can get out of here.'

'Nice to meet you, Kyle,' Jackson remarked. Although he was wearing full theatre garb, Jackson remained on the outer perimeter of the operating table.

'Likewise, sir.'

'Shouldn't that be Brilliant Surgeon?' she teased Kyle as she started suturing. 'After all, Jackson did agree to it.'

'No. That was what *you* were supposed to be calling him,' Kyle reasoned, and Susie smiled beneath her mask.

'Oh, yes. I forgot.' She glanced over at Jackson. 'I take it coffee was served without a hitch?'

'Yes.'

'Good.' There was silence for a while as Susie and Kyle continued with their work.

'It must have been a good evening,' Kyle said. 'At least, judging from Susie's flash hairstyle that's now hidden beneath her theatre cap.'

'It was,' Jackson replied, his gaze meeting Susie's for a few seconds.

'Right. We're done,' Susie announced, forcing herself to look away. She nodded to the anaesthetist before heading out of Theatre. She degowned and took a deep breath. Jackson followed her, removing his own theatre garb as well. 'So why did you really come down here?' she asked as she headed into the tearoom to write up the notes. When he didn't reply, she stopped and turned around, unsure whether he was still there. He collided with her, his hands instinctively resting on her waist to control his balance.

'Sorry,' she mumbled, and lifted her chin to gaze up at him. They were standing just inside the door to the empty tearoom and Susie didn't know whether she wanted it to fill up or stay deserted. 'I wasn't sure if you were…still…' Her voice trailed off. Aware that Jackson hadn't removed his hands from her body, his touch burned through the blue cotton of her theatre scrubs, making Susie intensely aware of their close proximity.

She felt a smouldering fire within her body come to life. Her breathing became shallow, her lips parting to allow the air to escape.

His blue eyes were clouded with desire, his breathing as uneven as her own. 'Why did I really come?' he asked. They were close, so close that his breath caressed her cheek as he spoke. He smelt good—too good, the scent of him only exacerbating the weakness of her knees.

'Susie, I won't lie to you.' He paused. 'And I can't deny it.'

'Deny what?' She held her breath, waiting for his answer.

'I'm attracted to you.' He raised one hand to gently cup her face, his thumb lightly brushing her parted lips. Susie's eyelids fluttered closed for an instant at his touch but she quickly opened them again.

This shouldn't be happening! She should be resisting him—but she was finding it, oh, so hard. As the day had worn on, Susie had found it increasingly difficult to control her reaction to Jackson, and here he was, standing right in front of her admitting he was attracted to her! Although the feelings were mutual, did she really want to get herself into this?

'We can't,' she choked out, but found herself powerless to move away.

'I know you feel it, too,' he continued.

'Yes.' The word came out as a groan as his head started to dip even closer to her own. He was so handsome. So wonderful. So sexy. The sexiest man she'd ever known. And here she was, in his arms, waiting desperately for him to kiss her. She'd *never* given in to feelings such as these before. Her previous relationships had all been conducted in a sane and logical manner. Slow and steady was her way. Not like this. Not jumping in with both feet. Not caring if she drowned. Not with a married man. She hardly knew him but the physical pull was just too strong to be ignored.

Jackson looked down into her face and saw confusion mixed with desire. She was obviously fighting the attraction as much as he was. He glanced at her lips, so full, so luscious, just waiting for him to kiss them.

He wanted to kiss her. He'd wanted to ever since they'd first met in her office. He instinctively knew she'd taste sweet—gloriously sweet—and that after he'd had one taste, he'd want more. The knowledge hit him hard and fast and he eased back a little. He'd been about to kiss another woman!

Jackson dropped his hands and stepped away. Susie swayed for a moment at the suddenness of his departure before recovering. She forced her wobbly knees to co-operate as she walked over to the table and sat down. She placed Mr Barnes's case notes on the table and opened them up to the operation notes. She stared at the blank page for a whole ten seconds, unable to recall anything she'd done during the operation.

She looked over at Jackson who was still standing in the doorway, raking an unsteady hand through his hair. 'I shouldn't have come,' he said, and he walked over and sat down opposite her.

'Probably,' she agreed.

'The fact remains that we'll be working closely together for the next five days. I don't want there to be any…bad feelings between us.'

Susie forced a smile. 'None. We can't help what we feel but we can control it.'

'True.' He stood. 'So I will leave you to write up your operation notes and see you for ward round tomorrow morning.'

'See you then,' she replied, but the look he gave her just before he walked out of the room told her that controlling their mutual attraction would be easier said than done.

Later, as Susie brushed her teeth before climbing into bed, she reflected on what an up-and-down sort of day she'd just had. In her mind, she could clearly hear her father saying, 'Most days just run one into the other and then, out of nowhere, comes a day that can change your life for ever.'

'Oh, Dad,' Susie whispered into the night. 'You're so right.' Her mind was full of mixed-up emotions. Happiness, confusion, excitement, anticipation…and guilt. What on earth would happen tomorrow? She closed her eyes, wondering whether she'd ever get to sleep.

It seemed only five minutes later that her alarm started to buzz and Susie reached out a hand to switch it off. She peered through her lashes at the digital display. Six-thirty. Time to rise and shine.

She stretched languorously in her bed, remembering the dream she'd had. She'd been at the snow with her family, enjoying toboggan rides with her nieces and nephews. Suddenly the children had changed to become her own children—a boy with short dark hair and blue eyes like his father, and a little girl with a mop of auburn curls like her mother.

Susie had laughingly slid down the mountain with her children on the toboggan—to their father who was waiting for them. When they'd finally come to a stop, two big strong hands had reached down to help both children out before they'd come to her aid as well. Two big strong hands that had secured themselves around her waist as she'd tilted her head up for a loving kiss. Two big strong hands whose touch still burned against her skin, causing goose-bumps to cascade over her body.

Jackson's hands!

Susie sat bolt upright in bed, her eyes as wide as saucers. Her heart was thumping rapidly against her chest and she felt a sheen of perspiration bead her forehead. What was she doing, dreaming about Jackson Myers? The man was becoming much too intrusive in her thoughts when he had no right to be.

He was only here for another five days. 'Five days!' she told herself aloud as disbelief turned to anger. She shoved the bedcovers aside and stomped to the bathroom. Wrenching on the shower taps, Susie allowed the spray of the hot water to calm her down. 'You can do this,' she told her reflection as she dried her hair. 'You're a professional. Just go to the hospital, smile politely at him, do your work and just…just concentrate on…on…' She desperately thought of something else to think about before the answer hit her. 'Your research.'

How had he managed to do it? For the past six months, since her last engagement had been terminated, Susie had focused solely on her work. She had refused dates and had even avoided going out in a group. At least since Greg had left the hospital for a job in Sydney, people had stopped giving her pitying looks.

And now there was Jackson. Within twenty-four hours he'd managed to make her feel extremely feminine and vulnerable. He was so charming. His manners were faultless and yet…she'd noticed a sadness creep into his eyes every now and then. She was intrigued by him and it was the last thing she wanted to be.

Susie switched off the hair-dryer and stared at her reflection, eyeing her features critically. He'd said she was beautiful and breathtaking. She wouldn't call herself beautiful. In her opinion, her eyes were crooked, her nose was too straight, her hair too curly and her mouth was… No, she conceded, her eyebrows creasing into a frown. She liked her mouth. She'd liked the way Jackson had caressed her lips with his thumb. Had liked it far too much. She recalled how she'd trembled deep inside, desperate for his lips to caress her in exactly the same way.

'No.' She spoke the word out loud. How he made her feel was…irrelevant. 'Remember that,' she warned herself as she clipped her hair back at the nape of her neck. Not for the first time Susie growled at her hair. Straight hair—she'd give anything for it!

Breakfast was next but she found she couldn't stomach much. She never could eat properly when she was distracted. Telling herself the cause of her uneasiness *wasn't* because she was going to see Jackson but because he and his team would be joining her ward round that morning, she quickly drank some orange juice and forced herself to eat a piece of toast before heading to the hospital.

When she arrived, she made sure her cool, calm and collected professional façade was in place as she walked to her office. 'Good morning, Todd,' she said as she breezed through the door.

'Well, hello. Aren't you looking like the consummate professional today?' her secretary teased. She'd dressed in one of her 'power' suits—navy trousers and jacket, white shirt and a silk vest.

'Thank you, thank you,' she replied as she quickly flicked through her in-tray. She had five minutes before she needed to head to the ward so she dealt with some paperwork before returning it to Todd.

'Gee, thanks,' he muttered, and she smiled sweetly at him. 'Off to ward round?'

'Yes.'

'Nervous?'

'Who, me?' she joked, and reached for her stethoscope. 'There's nothing else I have to do this morning? No more speeches? Introductions?'

'No. As far as Jackson's schedule is concerned, he's accompanying you on the ward round and then he's back off to the lecture theatre. You're in clinic this afternoon whilst he's lecturing to the fourth- and sixth-year medical students. Dinner this evening is sponsored by the Orthopaedic Bone Register and Research Foundation at the hotel Jackson is staying at.'

'Great. Thanks. Page me if you need me,' she told him as she headed out of the department. The closer she got to the ward, the tighter her stomach twisted into knots. She was going to see Jackson. Would she feel the same immediate connection again? Perhaps it had been a one-time thing?

When Susie entered the ward, she felt as though she was going to be physically sick, her stomach was churning so much. She took a deep breath and pushed open the door to the discussion room, where everyone congregated for the ward round meetings, only to find Jackson and his team weren't in there.

Several medical students, interns, physiotherapists and nurses turned to look at her.

Some murmured greetings and Susie politely returned them. There were more people than usual and she frowned, knowing it was because of Jackson. Everyone wanted to learn, watch and absorb everything he did during his time here. It would make for a slower ward round, but it couldn't be helped. After all, this was a teaching hospital.

'There you are, Susie,' the CNC said as she came bustling in. 'I've just received a call from Todd who wanted you to know Professor Myers and his team are stuck in traffic.'

Susie took a deep breath and let it out slowly. 'Thank you.' What should she do now? Should she wait to see if they arrived within the next ten minutes or should she start without them? As a general rule, ward round started on time, regardless of who was or wasn't there.

Susie followed the Clinical Nurse Consultant back to her desk and reached for the phone. 'Todd?' she said a moment later. 'More information, please.'

'There's a car crash on Gilchrist Avenue that's blocking traffic. Are you going to wait for them?'

'I'm not sure. What do you think?'

'They could be there in five minutes or five hours.'

'You're right. We can't keep the patients waiting all day. If Jackson misses the entire ward round, he can just join tomorrow's. I mean, it's not as if we have one ward round a week. We have them every morning!'

'Who are you trying to convince?' Todd said with a laugh.

'Keep me informed of the situation.'

'Will do.'

Susie replaced the receiver. 'Thank you,' she said to the CNC. 'I'll be starting the ward round on time, Sister.'

'Of course, Doctor,' the CNC replied with a nod. Susie returned to the discussion room where people were talking quite animatedly about the turn of events. She was swamped with questions as soon as she walked through the door.

'Is Professor Myers coming today or not?' one nurse asked.

'I have no idea. He's stuck in traffic. We'll be starting the round on time, though.'

'But you can't,' another complained.

'Yeah. This is my day off and I've specifically come in to watch him.'

'So have I.'

'I've cancelled a meeting,' someone else said.

'Well, I'm sorry but I can't control peak-hour traffic any more than Professor Myers can,' Susie stated. This wasn't a good beginning to the day. 'We'll be starting the ward round in...' she glanced at her watch '...three minutes. Thank you.'

She walked out and headed to the ward kitchen. She needed coffee—and fast. She made herself half a cup and drank it down before returning to the discussion room to start the round.

Some of the people who had come in on their day off left. That was their choice. As they went from patient to patient, Susie kept checking the doorway, hoping Jackson and his team would arrive.

They were halfway through the round when she looked up, straight into a pair of blue eyes that instantly melted her insides. Jackson! His silent arrival threw her off guard and she faltered for a second but quickly managed to recover.

As they moved on to the next patient, Susie took the opportunity of announcing his presence. 'Glad you could finally make it, Professor Myers.' Several people turned to look at him. He merely nodded, not a smile in sight. 'I take it this morning's traffic jam will ensure you don't forget Brisbane in a hurry,' she said lightly, and a few people chuckled. 'And now we come to Mrs Hammond. How are you this morning?' she asked her patient.

'Not bad, not bad, dearie. Got a bigger crowd than usual, I see.'

'Yes.' Susie smiled back and started her spiel on Mrs Hammond's injuries. Susie's stomach was knotted up again and she worked hard to control her involuntary emotional response to Jackson. Yesterday hadn't been imagined. It had been real. Very real.

After they'd finished the round, they returned to the discussion room where Susie usually answered questions, as well as asking a few herself. She wasn't at all surprised when many people asked their questions of Jackson and she was pleased when he checked with her before answering them.

Mindful of Jackson's tight schedule, Susie checked her watch and called for a final three questions. He shot her a grateful look. Almost one minute later Richard appeared in the doorway, ready to wrap things up, and Susie was pleased with herself for anticipating him. She was starting to feel in control of her emotions, telling herself it wasn't because of Jackson's presence.

As people starting filing out of the room, Richard came further in. 'I need to speak to you,' he said, his tone carrying a hint of annoyance. He headed over to Jackson, leaving Susie wondering what on earth she'd done wrong.

Jackson was still talking to a few people and Susie needed to check on Mr Barnes who was still in the critical care unit under close supervision. 'I need to check on a patient and then I'll be in my office,' she told Richard.

He nodded before politely interrupting Jackson's conversation. Susie left, trying to figure out what was going on as she headed to CCU. Mr Barnes's compartment syndrome was showing no signs of returning and Susie was pleased with his progress. He would need to have his drains taken out in a few days' time. She wrote up her notes, releasing Mr Barnes back to the orthopaedic ward, before heading to her office. No sooner had she sat in her chair than her door opened and an angry-looking Richard stormed in.

'I wasn't at all impressed, Susie.'

'With what?' she asked, feeling her hackles begin to rise. She stood to confront him.

'You started the ward round without Jackson!'

'What else was I supposed to do? Wait for him?' She walked around her desk and stood in front of him.

'He *is* the visiting orthopaedic professor,' Richard pointed out.

'Who just happened to be stuck in a traffic jam. It wasn't my fault, Richard. Besides, if it means that much to him, he can come tomorrow. We have ward rounds every morning, Richard.'

'But he was scheduled to come *this* morning.'

'And he did.'

'You still could have waited.'

'No, Richard. I couldn't. Firstly, I have patients who are in hospital for treatment. That means physio and OT appointments. It means social workers calling on them. Time for their family and friends to visit. Meals need to be served. Blood tests and X-ray appointments need to be organised. If ward round is late, everything else is thrown off for the rest of the day. Secondly, I was also trying to keep to Jackson's own schedule which you're so rigid about adhering to.'

Richard opened his mouth but Susie was all fired up. After all, she was a redhead and once she got going it was hard to stop her. 'Don't you even think of blaming me for this morning. I had no control over Jackson being late and just because you're angry and frustrated, it doesn't mean you can look at me for your scapegoat. Accept the situation, Richard. Accept that the ward round started without Jackson.'

'But it was down on his schedule that he was to take the ward round.'

'*Take* the ward round? No. Your schedule was *wrong*. As far as I was concerned, Jackson was merely joining *my* ward round. I'm in charge of that ward, Richard. Not you, not Jackson. If I'm away, the job falls to my senior registrar, Kyle Thompson. As a visiting dignitary, surely Jackson would realise that he has no real say in the treatment of my patients.'

'I do realise that,' Jackson said from the doorway, and both Susie and Richard turned to look at him. Neither of them had heard him enter and she wondered how long he'd been standing there. His words made her feel a little better but she was still angry with the way the entire morning had been handled.

'I'm glad to hear it,' she snapped.

'Why are you angry with me?'

'Because Richard is a member of your team. You should have made it clear to him that you weren't *taking* my ward round and that, regardless of your impromptu delay this morning, I still had a round to start on time.'

'You're right,' Jackson said as he crossed the room to stand before her. 'Richard, go and check things out in the lecture theatre.'

Susie could tell from his expression that he wasn't pleased with the way Richard had handled the situation.

'Aren't you coming?'

'I'll be there.' Jackson gave him a look that brooked no argument and Richard scuttled out of her office, closing the door behind him. 'I apologise, Susie. Not only on Richard's behalf but for myself as well. I had no idea he was going to take you to task over this morning's debacle.'

Susie was still standing in the middle of her office, her hands planted firmly on her hips. At his soft tone, she felt her anger dissolve. His ability to defuse her temper caused warning bells to ring inside her head. She lowered her hands to her side and quickly turned to walk behind her desk. 'Thank you,' she replied as she picked up a few papers from her in-tray.

When he didn't move, she glanced back up at him. 'Something else?'

'Yes. Thanks for allowing me to participate in your ward round.' His smile was encompassing. 'I know you wouldn't normally get that many people for a Tuesday morning ward round.'

'That's all right,' she said with a small smile. 'Some of them left when they found out you were going to be delayed.'

'Well, at least that was some consolation.' Jackson shook his head and started to pace slowly up and down in front of her desk. 'It's been a very strange morning. A traffic jam. A car accident, to be more precise, and Richard had one of his fits when I got out of the car to see if I could help. Thankfully, no one was badly injured so I returned to the car.' He tugged at the knot of his tie. 'Sometimes I wonder why I'm putting myself through this.'

'What? Wearing a tie?' she joked, hoping to lift the serious frown that now creased his brow. He stopped pacing and looked at her, the corners of his mouth twitching up slightly.

'You know what I mean. Just between you, me and the gatepost, I'm sick and tired of being handled all the time. It took a while to get used to and most of the time I can accept it, but on mornings such as these, when things are out of our control, Richard goes off on one of his tangents.' Jackson raked his hand through his hair and then shook his head. 'I probably shouldn't be talking to you about it. Sorry. I didn't mean to burden you with my problems.'

She didn't comment. She didn't *want* his confidences. It was too…personal and that was the last thing she needed.

He stared into her blue eyes. The tension between them was so…palpable, it scared her. She didn't want this. She didn't want to become involved. Regardless of how he made her feel, he would be leaving at the end of the week. She refused to be hurt again. *She didn't want this!*

'I'd better go,' he said abruptly, breaking eye contact. Susie looked away as well, dragging in a deep breath.

'Yes.'

He walked over to the door and then stopped, turning to look at her. 'Are you coming up to the lecture theatre now?'

'Ah…' she stalled, knowing she should as his lecture was due to start within the next few minutes. 'I'll be along directly.'

Without another word, he left her office and Susie slumped down into her chair with relief.

'Pull yourself together,' she told herself. She tried to focus her thoughts on the work in front of her but her mind refused to budge from how incredible Jackson made her feel. With one glance, she was lost. 'This can't be happening.' She buried her face in her hands.

Only this time it was different. Different from Walter and different from Greg. Or was it? Was she just telling herself that in order to justify her feelings? She hadn't listened to the warning bells that had gone off when Greg had cancelled three of their dates in a row in order to work. What work? They worked at the same hospital, albeit in different departments, but still she had justified his behaviour. Afterwards, she'd discovered he'd been having affairs.

'Hindsight,' she said out loud. 'Learn from it.' But the way Jackson had looked at her last night had been the way she'd yearned for a man to look at her. She'd never thought of herself as beautiful, average perhaps but not stunningly beautiful, yet whenever Jackson had gazed at her it had made her feel as though she were the most desirable woman in the world.

'Susie!' Todd's voice made her spring up from her chair and glare at him standing by the door. 'You're supposed to be upstairs. What are you doing, sleeping at your desk?'

'I wasn't sleeping,' she said defensively as she headed towards him. 'I was deep in thought and you scared me.'

'Good. Now, get upstairs before I have Richard annoying me by sending out a search party for you.'

'I don't know why it should matter whether I'm a few minutes late. I'm not introducing him today. I'll just sneak in up the back and no one will notice.'

'Jackson will,' he pointed out, and she knew it to be true. She didn't want Jackson to think she wasn't interested in what he had to say, because she was. When she arrived, he was just walking to the podium and she quickly sat down in one of the back seats. He looked up, his gaze melding with hers, as though he'd instinctively known where she was sitting, and her heart slammed wildly against her ribs.

Taking a breath, he began his talk, his gaze now roving over the audience before him. Susie found herself completely drawn in as he explained and illustrated, with the help of colour slides, a new technique that could be adapted for both hip and knee arthroplasties.

Afterwards, he was again inundated with questions and answered them patiently. He was brilliant. Handsome, successful, brilliant—and married.

Susie returned to her office and collected her bag before heading to the restaurant across the street where they'd again be having lunch. This time there were only about thirty people joining them and they were shown through to a smaller function room.

'I didn't think you'd make it,' Jackson told her as he held her chair. Susie sat and waited for him to be seated as well.

'Sorry about that.'

'No need to apologise. I thought an emergency might have come up after I'd left.'

'Nothing so justifiable.' Susie paused for a moment, deciding whether to continue. Feeling her blood pumping furiously around her body, making her light-headed, she said, 'I'm ashamed to admit I was…lost in thought.' She cleared her throat, unable to quite believe she'd said what she had.

Jackson leaned a little closer. 'I hope it was a…pleasant diversion.'

Susie edged back slightly, a curious smile tugging at her lips. 'Are you flirting with me, Professor Myers?'

His eyes widened at her words but he nodded slowly. 'Feels a lot like it, from what I can recall.'

Richard interrupted them, handing Jackson his notes for yet another short speech. Susie was glad of the reprieve as she tried to understand what Jackson had just said. 'From what I can recall.' What was that supposed to mean?

She reached out and filled her water glass.

'Don't choke,' he said softly as he rose to his feet.

Soon, everyone was clapping after Jackson's speech, and their meal was being served. The person seated to her left was a theatre nurse she'd worked with several times, and the two of them talked about a variety of topics.

Just as coffee was being served, Susie checked her watch and gasped when she realised the time.

'Something wrong?' Jackson asked, a frown on his face.

'If I don't run, I'll be late for clinic.' She took a quick sip of her coffee.

'I'll walk back with you,' he stated.

'That's not necessary.' She drained her cup and stood. 'Besides, it will take you ages to get out of here. Everyone wants to have a word with you.'

'Well, they'll have to wait. I need to have a word with you.'

'Oh.' Susie wasn't quite sure what to say. Had she done something wrong again? She edged towards the doorway as the nurse who'd been sitting beside her asked Jackson a question.

'Will you be at the dinner this evening?' he asked her, and she nodded. 'How about we catch up then? Sorry to do this but I'm running late for an important meeting and then I'm lecturing again this afternoon.'

'We'll talk at dinner, then,' the nurse replied soothingly, her eyes saying that she wanted to do more than talk to him. Susie felt sick. She was out of the restaurant and heading towards the pedestrian crossing when Jackson caught up with her.

'I thought I said I'd walk back with you.'

'From the look of things, you were otherwise engaged.'

'What are you talking about?'

'Forget it,' she said, angry with him for not knowing when women were literally throwing themselves at him. Surely an attractive man of his age knew how to reel in the females. She shook her head. He was no different to Greg. Greg, who'd had affairs with almost every nurse in the hospital! Greg, who'd had such an easy, charming manner with the women and had used it to his best advantage. Well, she wasn't going to be taken in by another womaniser.

'So what did you want to talk about?' she asked as the pedestrian light turned green. She headed off across the road with Jackson at her side, each as huffy as the other.

'I wanted to talk about what's going on between us.'

'What?' Susie stopped and gazed incredulously at him. As far as she was concerned, they'd put an end to it last night as both of them had agreed to keep their distance. Jackson grabbed her arm and propelled her along.

'Stopping in the middle of the road isn't a wise idea, Susie.' He let go of her arm as soon as they reached the other side, both of them continuing towards the hospital. 'I know you feel the same pull of emotion I do. It happens every time we get within sight of each other.'

Susie opened the side door leading to a staircase that came out near her office. Jackson followed her, their footsteps echoing off the walls.

When they came out in the department, she headed up the corridor and went directly into her office. She held the door for him and closed it the instant he was inside.

'Now, what is this all about?' she asked. Her chest was starting to ache from her increased breathing, and after the confrontations she'd already had this morning she didn't thank Jackson for providing her with another one.

Jackson didn't stop walking and paced restlessly around her floor. 'I need to tell you something, Susie.'

'What?' She made no attempt to move, still standing by the door. He came over and took her hands in his, leading her over to a chair.

'Sit down.'

'I don't want to sit down,' she retorted, but stood with the backs of her knees pressing against the chair.

'Can you feel that?' His voice was harsh yet urgent. 'When I touch your hands? It's there, Susie. Whatever this thing is between us, it's there.'

'So? We don't have to act on it. You'll be gone at the end of the week and—'

'Susie.' He dropped her hands and took a few steps away. His actions were stiff and unnatural. Something was *really* wrong. 'We need to talk.'

'About what? About this attraction?'

'No. About my wife.'

CHAPTER FOUR

SUSIE'S mouth hung open and she stared at him with incredulity as she dropped down onto the chair.

'Your *wife*? I don't want to hear about your wife!'

Jackson exhaled harshly and raked an unsteady hand through his hair as he started to pace the room again.

She watched his movements, trying not to admire his long legs. Here she was, having a multitude of amorous emotions about the man, yet all he wanted was to talk about his marriage, like she was some sort of counsellor. The anger started building inside and she narrowed her eyes, glaring at him.

'How dare you even talk about an attraction between us? I won't become involved with a married man and don't you dare even ask me.' As her words penetrated her own mind, she laughed humourlessly. 'What am I saying? You'll be gone at the end of the week and any unwanted romantic yearnings will be going with you.' She shook her head. 'Married.' She watched him pace and realised that his agitation was increasing.

She slowly stood, quickly leaning on her desk as she realised her legs weren't quite up to supporting her yet. She manoeuvred around to her chair and thankfully sat down again.

'Right. Finished? Good,' he said, not waiting for an answer. 'I don't have a wife.'

Susie frowned. 'What?'

'I don't have a wife.'

'But you said—'

'I said I wanted to tell you about my wife.'

The wheels started turning slowly. 'So you're not married?'

'I'm a widower,' he said softly, and Susie's anger evaporated into thin air.

'Oh, Jackson.' It explained a lot. Why he seemed oblivious when women were flirting with him. Why he was always polite and attentive. Why the expression in his eyes changed from one of desire to one of confusion in an instant.

Susie stared at him. He looked so lost...so desolate. She wanted to go to him and wrap her arms about him—but she didn't. Even though he'd shared this with her, she still didn't know him and he was, after all, a colleague. A colleague who would only be here for another five days! How many times did she have to keep reminding herself of that?

Quite a few, it seemed, as she couldn't deny she was drawn to him. She didn't understand it and was finding it increasingly difficult to control.

'When did she die?'

'Almost eighteen months ago.' He shoved his hands into his pockets and looked down at the ground. 'Alison was my secretary for about a year before we were married. It was her idea to do the VOP and, in fact, she arranged most of it.'

Susie nodded slowly. That explained why his dossier said he was married. He'd felt obliged to continue with the VOP to fulfil his wife's dream.

'Alison died suddenly in a road accident six months before the VOP was due to begin. She was supposed to come with me on the tour.' Jackson looked at Susie, his face blank. His words were delivered without emotion and Susie realised that he still missed his wife very much.

'You don't need to explain anything to me,' she said softly.

'I wanted you to know.'

'I appreciate it.'

Jackson stood where he was, closer to the door than to her desk. His gaze encompassed her and Susie worked hard to control her heart rate. He might be a widower but he had another woman in his heart.

Even as she told herself this, she couldn't stop the way her body reacted to him. Her pulse had increased, her breathing was now more rapid and her stomach was back to churning with repressed desire. With a single glance, Jackson was able to affect her. It wasn't fair.

The air in the room seemed to grow thick with suppressed tension and Susie knew she couldn't look away. Not this time. He had shared a most intimate part of himself with her.

The beeper attached to the waistband of his trousers sounded. Jackson checked the number and rolled his eyes. 'May I?' He gestured to her phone. He punched in the number on his pager and waited impatiently. 'Yes, Richard?' he answered. 'I'll be right there.'

The short reprieve had been enough for Susie to collect her thoughts. Part of her felt liberated. Jackson wasn't married. She didn't need to feel guilty any more about her attraction to him.

He smiled at her. A small lopsided grin that had her heart rate picking up. 'I'll see you tonight. At dinner.'

'Ah…yes.' Susie returned his smile before watching him leave. As soon as he'd shut her door, she buried her head in her hands again. Making little sobbing noises, she wondered how she found herself in these sorts of situations. She was attracted to Jackson and although he would only be here for five days, which was enough motivation for her to keep away from him, to compound the situation even more, he was a widower. A widower who was apparently still in love with his wife.

'Are you sleeping again?' Todd said as he walked up to her desk. 'If you weren't the boss, I'd be reporting you.'

Susie looked up at him, too exhausted to hide her emotions. 'What's wrong?' Todd asked instantly.

Susie sighed. 'Oh, nothing. It just hasn't been the best of days so far.'

'Does it have anything to do with Jackson?' Todd asked, and Susie looked at him sharply.

'What do you mean?'

'Other people don't know you as well as I do.'

'Meaning?' Susie said, encouraging him to say more.

'That I know you're attracted to Jackson and, judging by the way he was acting last night, waiting impatiently for you to arrive, I'd say he's just as attracted to you.'

'You're right,' Susie said dejectedly.

'So why don't you go for it?'

'Huh. You know my history with men.'

'Jackson isn't Greg, Susie. Or Walter. You shouldn't tar all of us with the same brush.'

'Why not?'

'I take offence at that,' he replied half-jokingly.

'Sorry. It would never work.'

'Why? Because he's a widower?'

'You know?'

'Sure. Richard told me.'

'Why didn't you——?' She stopped. 'Never mind.' She stared out into nothingness before shrugging. 'It just wouldn't work. Too many complications.' She took a deep breath and pasted on a smile. 'So I'm going to put it out of my mind and get to clinic.' She glanced at the clock on the wall. 'Oh, my goodness. I didn't realise the time. I'm late already.'

'That's what I came in to tell you.'

'Fine assistant you are,' she chided, but grew serious as she came around her desk. 'Thanks, Todd.'

'Get going.'

Susie rushed to clinic, greeting the patients as she walked through the crowded waiting room. During the clinic, she hardly had time to draw breath, let alone dwell on thoughts relating to Jackson Myers. When she was on the second last patient, the phone on her consulting desk shrilled to life.

'Dr Monahan,' she said absent-mindedly into the receiver as she wrote up notes.

'Hi, Susie. It's Mallory.'

'Oh, hi. Long time, no hear.' Susie had worked with Mallory's husband, Nick Sterling, years ago, and after Nick had introduced her to Mallory, the two had become good friends. 'How is everyone?'

'Just fine. Edward's had a bit of a hay fever but, then, it is spring so it's to be expected. Listen, Todd told me you were in clinic so I won't keep you long. Nick and I were hoping to get down to Brisbane during the week to catch up with the visiting professor, but it's just been one emergency after the other. Todd told me that Jackson doesn't have anything planned for Saturday and we were wondering if he'd like to take a break from hotels and restaurant meals to come up here for a bit of home cooking.'

'You're cooking?' Susie jested.

'No.' She could tell Mallory was smiling. 'Arlene will be cooking. Oh, you know what I mean. It won't be restaurant food. You could drive him up and that way, we can catch up with you, too.'

Susie thought for a moment. The drive to the Sunshine Coast where Nick and Mallory lived was only one hour away, but the thought of being confined in a car with Jackson for the drive there and back made Susie catch her breath.

'I'm not sure, Mallory.'

'Well, I'm sure he'd like the chance to meet Nick, you know, as Nick also did a visiting professorship. Granted, it was in general surgery but, still, the same sort of schedule applies.'

'Oh, I can see why you'd both want to meet Jackson but I don't know whether I'll be able to come. Perhaps he'd feel more comfortable hiring a car and driving there by himself. Appleton is very beautiful in the spring.'

'Except when you have a three-year-old with hay fever,' Mallory joked.

'Is Rebekah still enjoying school?' Susie asked in a bid to change the subject for a moment.

'She loves it. She's eight years old and knows absolutely everything. She's always right, and as her father is of the same opinion and temperament, it makes for interesting...discussions.' Mallory laughed.

'I can well believe it. Look, I'll run the idea past Jackson this evening at dinner and let you know.'

'Thanks. That would be great.'

When Susie had hung up, she shook her head slowly. Her relationship with Jackson must remain strictly professional. If she were to accompany him to Appleton, as well as introducing him to her close friends, it would be more of a personal relationship. It was too tempting. Far too tempting.

There was a knock at her door and Susie snapped out of her reverie. 'Susie, have you got a minute to look at some X-rays? I'd like your opinion,' Kyle said after opening her door.

'Back to business,' she mumbled, and walked over to where Kyle was hooking the radiographs up onto the viewer. Work was definitely one way to keep her mind off Jackson and she was thankful for a job that required so much of her concentration. They managed to finish the clinic just after five-thirty, which was only half an hour late. Susie wrote up the last of the notes as Kyle stopped and said good-night to her. 'Are you coming to the dinner tonight?' she asked.

'After missing last night's dinner? I'll definitely be there.'

'See you then, Kyle.' She returned her attention to the notes but heard Kyle's voice in the distance talking to someone. The nurses had left the instant the last patient had departed so Susie wondered who it might be.

Seconds later, she heard footsteps heading towards her consulting room and looked up expectantly at the open doorway.

'Hi,' Jackson said a moment later. 'I hope I'm not disturbing you?'

Susie's heart lurched happily at the sight of him and a shiver of excited anticipation worked its way down her spine. Yes, he *was* disturbing her—far too much for her liking. 'No. I'm just finishing up.' She motioned to the notes, all the while trying to calm herself.

'Don't let me interrupt,' he said, and looked at some of the posters stuck up on the wall. Susie quickly finished writing the notes and the instant she'd closed the file and put her pen down her phone rang.

'Excuse me,' she said, but Jackson merely nodded. 'Dr Monahan.'

'Susie, an emergency has just come in. They're demanding the head of the unit,' Triage Sister said.

Susie groaned resignedly. 'Details?'

'Right scapula, right Colles' and dislocation of the neck of humerus. Susie, it's Blade Fargo.'

'Is that name supposed to mean something to me?'

'Honestly, Susie. Don't you ever go to the movies?'

'Sure. So?' She glanced at Jackson, only to find him watching her.

'Problem?' he said softly.

'Emergency,' she mouthed, and he nodded.

'Blade Fargo is the hottest thing in movies,' Triage Sister was saying. '*Cool Pets*? *Everybody's Hero*? The remake of *Swan Song*?'

'Oh, yeah. I've seen that one. Right.' Susie at least had a picture of the actor in her head.

'He's been filming his latest film in several locations around Brisbane and today they were doing a stunt and he fell.'

'At least he wasn't playing sport,' she mumbled.

'Pardon?'

'Nothing. I'm on my way.' She hung up the receiver and turned her attention to Jackson.

'What's happening?'

'Blade Fargo is in A and E.'

'Who?'

Susie laughed again. 'I'm glad to see I'm not the only one out of touch. He's a movie star,' she continued as she packed up her desk and headed for the door. Turning out her light, she looked over her shoulder at him. 'Want to accompany me to A and E?'

'Sure.' His enthusiasm was evident.

'I guess most of the operating you've done has been scheduled.'

'Exactly. I can't recall the last time I dealt with an emergency.'

Susie pressed the button for the lift and while they waited she tilted her head and eyed him thoughtfully. 'What's the deal with your operating and practising licence? You must have operated in some of the finest facilities in the world.'

'I have. For visiting professorships, the recipient is granted an international operating licence.'

'So you could quite easily operate with me right now if I asked you.'

'Yes.' The lift arrived and they rode it down to A and E. 'Will you?' he asked with the delighted anticipation of a child at Christmas. 'Please?'

Susie couldn't help but smile at him. 'I don't know.' She pretended to consider him thoughtfully. 'How's your upper-limb expertise?'

'Pretty rusty,' he confessed. 'But I'd only be assisting,' he was quick to point out.

'Let's see how his injuries present. Chances are, he won't require surgery at all.' She told him what the triage sister had said and he nodded, all pretence gone as they walked into A and E. If she'd wanted to get people's attention, she had it—walking in with the visiting orthopaedic professor to treat a movie star.

The noise coming from outside was deafening and Security was stationed at the front door to the hospital as well as the door that led through to the treatment area.

'There you are, Susie,' Triage Sister said. 'He's in T2.'

'Thank you. What's going on?'

'Mr Fargo's fans!'

'Oh.' Susie shrugged and led the way to treatment room two. 'Hello,' she said to the patient lying on the bed. She did indeed recognise him now but he looked a lot smaller in real life. 'I'm Dr Monahan. Head of Orthopaedics. This is my colleague, Professor Myers.'

Blade Fargo nodded slightly and then winced in pain.

'Can't you people do something?' the woman standing next to him complained. 'He's in pain.'

Susie accepted the patient chart from one of the nurses and checked his analgesics. 'Are you still experiencing pain, Mr Fargo?'

'Blade,' he said softly.

'Any pain, Blade?'

'Minor.'

'You people have got to do something,' the woman shrilled again.

'I don't believe we've been introduced.' Susie spoke to the woman, a polite smile pasted in place.

The woman sighed with dramatic exasperation. 'I'm his manager. Now, do something.'

'I will,' Susie said. 'Unfortunately, you'll need to wait outside. The sister here will show you where.'

'I'm not leaving him.' The woman grabbed his hand and poor Blade cried out in pain. Still, he kept his cool.

'It's all right, Margo. I'll be in good hands.'

Margo looked at him and pouted. 'Sure, Bladey?'

'I'm sure,' he confirmed. 'Go and appease the fans.'

'Good thinking,' Margo replied, the pout gone. She straightened her shoulders and allowed herself to be led out of T2.

'Now, Mr Far— Blade,' Susie corrected herself. She moved in for a closer look at his injuries. 'Let's see what sort of damage has been done.' She inspected his arm gently before checking his other arm. He had a few cuts and scratches on his legs and upper torso which had been attended to by the A and E staff.

'I think we'll let Radiology enjoy your company next,' Susie said with a smile as she wrote up the X-ray request forms. 'You've dislocated your shoulder but I don't want to put it back in without it being X-rayed first.'

'Why not?' he asked.

'Because you may have fractured the top of your humerus, which is the upper arm bone. If you have, we'll need to operate to fix the pieces of bone together before relocating it.'

'If not?'

'Then I can put it back in.'

'Will it be painful?

Susie smiled. 'We'll make sure you have sufficient analgesics to cover the pain. Your Colles' fracture, which is your wrist, looks straightforward and can probably be fixed with a simple plaster cast.'

'I can't have a cast on my arm,' he stated in a normal voice. 'I'm right in the middle of shooting a movie. The hold-up of waiting for my arm to heal in a cast would cost the studio millions.'

'I'm sure they're covered for it,' Susie continued calmly.

'Can I get a second opinion?'

'Of course,' she replied, not at all offended. She could see where he was coming from and thought it only reasonable that he ask. 'First of all, let's see what the X-rays show and then we'll know exactly what we're dealing with.'

'Right you are, Doc,' he said, and smiled at her. He was a handsome man, Susie thought, but his looks were too...polished.

'You handled that well,' Jackson said once Blade had been wheeled off, with three adoring nurses at his side, towards Radiology.

'Why do you sound so surprised?' She laughed as she led him into the A and E tearoom. 'Coffee?'

'Thanks.'

'Black. No sugar, right?'

'How did you know?'

Susie chuckled. 'Let's see, since you arrived here I've already had three meals sitting next to you. I simply noticed you didn't add anything into your coffee before you drank it.'

He smiled at her. 'And you have two with moo.'

'I haven't heard that one before,' Susie replied as she brought two cups of coffee over.

'I was in Alice Springs just before I came here and heard one of the surgeons say it.'

'Happy to be back in the country?'

'Yes.' He took a sip of his coffee. 'Do you know, in the past few months, I've had a hankering for anything and everything Australian? Meat pies and tomato sauce. Lamingtons. Tim Tam biscuits. All the things that are hard to get overseas.' He leaned forward slightly and said in a conspiratorial whisper, 'I even watched some of the Australian TV soaps if they were on.'

Susie laughed. 'I know what you mean. I did an eighteen-month stint in Asia a few years ago and near the end, especially when you know that you'll soon be heading back home, you crave any small link with your home country.'

Jackson leaned back and stretched. 'And now, thanks to you, I have the opportunity to help out on an emergency call.'

His words were fuzzy in her ears as her gaze was drawn to the way his muscles flexed beneath his shirt when he stretched. It should be outlawed. He'd removed his suit jacket when they'd entered the tearoom and slung it over the back of a chair. His crisp, white shirt did nothing to hide what lay beneath and Susie's heart rate accelerated.

She quickly looked away in case he should intercept her gaze. What was she doing, ogling him like that? He was a man in love with another woman. Or, more correctly, the memory of another woman. How could she possible hope to compete with that? The thought struck her like a blow. Did she want to compete?

'Susie?' There was concern in his voice when he spoke.

'Sorry.' She forced herself to meet his gaze but she didn't hold it for long. Instead, she stood and walked over to the bench. Distance. She needed to put distance between them.

'Something wrong?'

'No. No. Nothing's wrong.' She shook her head for emphasis and then eyed him cautiously. 'Why do you ask?'

'No reason,' he stated. 'You just seemed miles away.'

'Ah...yes. Sorry about that.' What was wrong with her? She was behaving like an adolescent with a crush. Jackson stood and walked slowly towards her. Susie watched his progress, her breathing increasing with each step he took.

Finally, after what seemed like an eternity, he stood beside her. He leant against the bench and she could feel the warmth of his thigh pressing close to hers. Her eyelids fluttered closed momentarily as she savoured the brief contact.

'Susie...'

'Mmm?' Susie waited, holding her breath to see what he would say next.

'Are you...' he paused, '...seeing anyone at the moment?' He wasn't sure why he was asking her. Both of them knew that nothing should happen between them, but for some strange reason he had a burning need to know.

Her eyes snapped open and her breath whooshed out quickly as a delicious wave of excitement rippled through her at his words, one she found hard to control. 'Ah…no. No. My last engagement broke up six months ago.'

'I see.' She'd been engaged? The thought had never crossed his mind. It also drove home just how little he knew about her. 'Does he work here?'

'He did. He's in Sydney now.' Susie couldn't hide the pain she still felt at Greg's betrayal.

'He hurt you.' Jackson immediately felt incredibly protective towards her. How could any man treat this gorgeous and generous woman so badly?

'Yes. Greg hurt me.'

'I see.' This explained why she was fighting the attraction between them with all her might. She didn't want to risk getting hurt again and Jackson couldn't blame her. He felt the same way. It had taken Alison a while to work her way into his heart and then, after such a short time of happiness, she'd been taken from him. Love was cruel.

The tearoom door opened and a nurse came in, carrying a large packet of X-rays. 'Here you go, Susie.'

'Thanks.' Those precious few candid moments she and Jackson had shared dissipated into thin air. Work! Focus on your work. Susie forced her legs to move and headed over to the X-ray viewing box on the wall. She flicked the switch to illuminate it and hooked the first radiograph up.

'Dislocation looks clean,' she said as he joined her. He wasn't as close as he'd just been and for that she was grateful. She needed to concentrate and she was finding it increasingly difficult to do so with Jackson around. She changed the films. 'Ulna and radius require open reduction and internal fixation.'

'You'll need to reduce and relocate the Colles' as well,' Jackson pointed out. 'What do you think about bandaging and putting his arm in a splint?'

'We just need to keep everything stable,' she agreed with a nod.

'If you insert a few K-wires here…' Jackson pointed to the fracture site of Blade Fargo's right wrist '…that will hold the fracture in place.'

'I'd need to restrict him in the length of time he's out of the splint, and he'll require a nurse to handle the bandaging.'

'Absolutely.'

'What do you think? An hour a day?'

'At least for the first two weeks. Then once you get the check X-rays done, you may be able to extend that time frame or decrease it, depending on how things look.'

Susie nodded. 'Could be a workable solution. Let's see how we go in Theatre.' Not wanting to be alone with Jackson for too long, Susie gathered up the films and headed back to her patient.

'It looks as though we may have a solution to your problem,' Susie told Blade. 'But,' she added at his brilliant smile, 'you'll be under strict instructions as to how much you can do. And, please, no more stunts! Use the stuntman next time.'

'Yes, Doctor,' Blade said with mock remorse.

'I can't make any promises,' Susie said. 'It was Professor Myers's idea, so if it doesn't work out you can blame him for dashing your hopes.'

Jackson chuckled. Susie explained the operation to Blade, and once he'd signed the con-

sent form she headed to Theatre to get everything prepared. 'It's six-thirty now,' Susie said
to him. 'Unfortunately, it doesn't look as
though you'll have time to help me in Theatre.'

'Why not?'

'Jackson, you have a dinner at eight o'clock.
That's only an hour and a half away.'

'I do know how to tell the time,' he said
with an admonishing grin.

'Stop teasing.' Susie smiled, loving the way
they could interact like this. They were on the
same wavelength. Neither Walter nor Greg had
clicked with her so instantly. Perhaps that was
why she found him so hard to resist! 'Richard
will come looking for you and then you'll have
to leave in the middle of the operation.
Actually, I'm surprised he allowed you a few
free hours.'

Jackson chuckled. 'It'll be all right. The operation's going to take...what? Forty-five
minutes?'

'More than likely, but what if we run into
complications?'

'I seriously doubt it.'

'You have responsibilities.'

'I have an hour and a half. We'll be fine.'

The look he gave her said that she could
trust him and for a split second Susie won-

dered whether he was only talking about the operation or…something more. She decided it was best not to pursue it so she showed him where the changing rooms were and escaped behind the door marked FEMALES.

'You're a cool, calm and collected professional,' she mumbled to herself as she changed. 'You've been through a lot worse than this. It's just an attraction. Nothing is ever going to come of it. He's still carrying a torch for his wife and he's leaving at the end of the week. He has a tour to complete and even after that's done, he'll be living in a different state.'

'Talking to yourself again, Susie?' Patti, one of the nurses who'd been ogling Jackson the previous day, said as she walked in.

For a second, she froze. How much of her mumbling had Patti heard? Susie adopted an air of nonchalance and continued to put her hair up.

'So, another opportunity to work with the great Professor Myers,' Patti squeaked excitedly. '*And* assist with an operation for Blade Fargo. Is this the best job or what?'

Susie couldn't help but laugh. She didn't need to tell Patti to make sure she stayed professional. She might not have that much in common with the nurse but Patti was very good at her job.

'The only downside is that after tonight my contract with the hospital expires.'

'I didn't realise you were doing agency work. You've been here for at least three months.'

'I've been filling in for a nurse off on maternity leave. She's back as of tomorrow, which means I won't be around to...visit Blade.'

'Why don't you take a holiday? Enjoy some time off?'

Patti laughed. 'I think cleaning my apartment takes precedence over everything at the moment.'

'We'd better get going,' Susie said as she motioned towards the door.

'Sure.' They walked out together. 'How did you get Professor Myers to agree to operate?' Patti's question made Susie want to throw caution to the wind and say something like it had been her natural charms that had led Jackson away from his busy schedule in search of a more...refined amusement but instead she cleared her throat. Not wanting to create hospital gossip, she said, 'Firstly, *he* is assisting *me*. Secondly...' Susie shrugged. 'He asked.'

Susie checked on Blade to make sure that everything was going according to plan before she headed for the scrub sink. There was no sign of Jackson but she knew he'd arrive soon.

The hairs on the back of her neck and along her arms rose the moment he entered the room. She was amazed at how aware she was of him but tried to hide it as best she could.

As they stood at the scrub sink, he said, 'Everything ready to go?'

'Yes.'

'I called Richard,' he told her. 'So at least he knows where I am.'

Susie nodded, fiercely trying to concentrate on what she was doing. The theatre blues brought out the blueness of his eyes—eyes that she could willingly drown in. She glanced at his large, capable hands as he continued to lather them and his arms. So strong. So masterful. So…sensual.

This won't do! Susie returned her gaze to her own arms and hands, intent on focusing her thoughts on the upcoming operation. Thankfully, by the time the operation began, she was back in control of her emotions. Jackson was merely another surgeon, assisting her in her work.

They worked well together, relocating the shoulder and performing open reduction and internal fixation on the fractured radius and ulna. The K-wires that needed to be inserted into the wrist were another matter, yet together they worked it through, with both of them quite satisfied with the result.

'A job well done,' Jackson remarked as he pulled off his mask and theatre cap. Susie looked up at him and he smiled. Delight swamped her body again and she quickly turned away. She had to—if she was going to save her sanity!

CHAPTER FIVE

'SUSIE? Are you feeling all right?'

'Yes.' She dared a quick glance up at Jackson while she disposed of her theatre garb. 'I'd better write up the notes,' she mumbled, and quickly headed back to the tearoom, thankful that Jackson wasn't following her. He was probably changing back into his business suit or talking to staff.

Either way, she was glad of the momentary reprieve. She wrote up the notes but discovered she'd made two mistakes. It irked her when her mind wandered to Jackson. Susie corrected them before closing the case notes. Why did it irk her so much? Was it the fact that she was attracted to Jackson? Or the fact that she felt out of control whenever he was around? And what was wrong with feeling a little out of control once in a while?

She knew there could never be anything between them so why shouldn't she enjoy the way he made her pulse race? Or the way her stomach churned in excitement? It was definitely bolstering her bruised ego. Jackson found her desirable. After what Greg had done to her, she'd added some more baggage to her neuroses. So why shouldn't she be delighted with Jackson's attentions?

Walter, her first fiancé, had found her attractive but had only said so once. The day he'd broken their engagement. He'd been married to his work and when Susie had refused to forgo her study in favour of his ambition, Walter had broken the engagement.

'You're a beautiful woman, Susan Monahan,' Walter had said as he'd risen from the table they'd been eating at. 'You would have done my career proud.' With that, he'd turned and walked out of the restaurant—leaving her to pay the bill.

'What was I thinking?' she muttered. How had she allowed herself to be enamoured of first Walter and then Greg?

'Thought I'd find you here.' Jackson's voice washed over her and Susie momentarily closed her eyes, savouring the sound and the way it made her feel before opening her eyes and turning to look at him. He was dressed in his suit again, looking more handsome than before, if that was at all possible. 'I'd better get going.' He stayed in the doorway, not venturing any further.

Susie automatically looked at the clock, gasping as she saw the time. Ten minutes to eight. 'I'd completely forgotten about the dinner.'

He smiled. 'I thought as much. You are still coming?'

'Yes, but it appears I'm going to be a little late. As the dinner is at your hotel, it won't take you any time at all to change and get to the venue.'

'Whereas you need to go home, shower and change and then drive to the hotel,' he finished for her.

'Yes.'

'I'll save you a seat.'

Susie smiled. 'That's pretty decent of you—especially as the seating has already been organised.'

He returned her smile and she melted. 'See you there,' he said, before walking away. Susie sighed, the silly smile still on her face. You're not having much luck fighting your feelings, she told herself.

'Work,' she said, and stood, pushing thoughts of Jackson Myers out of her mind. She headed for Recovery to check on Blade, and when she was satisfied with his stable condition, she left the nurses to drool over their movie-star patient.

At home, she took a leisurely shower and dressed with extra care. She'd seen the slightly veiled looks of desire in Jackson's eyes the previous evening and tonight she wanted it again. He made her feel feminine, delicate and sexy—all at the same time. They were sensations she'd never felt before and she'd discovered, much to her chagrin, that she liked it!

Ever since she'd met Jackson yesterday morning, he'd been her constant companion— well, at least in her mind. Had it only been that long? Yet she couldn't stop thinking about him. In some respects, she felt as though she'd known him for years.

Susie smoothed her hand down the long burgundy silk dress she'd bought two weeks before. She'd bought it specifically for this occasion, as she'd done with all the dresses she'd wear this week. Prior to this, she hadn't given herself permission to spoil herself.

Tonight, instead of piling her curls on top of her head, she let them fall loose, adding a rhinestone clip to each side at the front to keep it out of her eyes. Vanilla essence was next, and she dabbed some on her wrists and behind her ears. Usually she wore perfume but tonight she wanted to…what? Leave a lasting impression on Jackson? Have him find her too good to resist?

'Just enjoy it,' she told her reflection. 'Nothing is going to happen and at least you'll have some nice memories to combat the awful ones.' With a firm nod, she collected her bag and keys before heading out the door.

Susie arrived just an hour late, but it was worth the wait. During the entrée, Jackson had found himself glancing at the door more often than not. The main course had been served and he'd asked a waiter to hold a meal for Dr Monahan, knowing she'd be hungry after such a long afternoon in clinic and then Theatre.

She finally arrived and the same reaction he'd experienced the night before hit him again. She was a vision of loveliness, dressed in a rich burgundy fabric that shimmered when she walked. Her hair was loose, except for two sparkling clips on either side. He had a sudden urge to thread his fingers through her glorious mane which shone reddish-gold beneath the artificial lights. He was amazed at how strongly she affected him, and although he'd done his best to fight it, he'd found he was losing the battle.

'Hey. Here's Susie,' Kyle announced, breaking into Jackson's intimate thoughts. He watched her look over as Kyle called her name and waved. She waved back and said something to the people who had waylaid her before heading over. She walked with such grace and poise, holding her shoulders back. She was one elegant lady.

Jackson waited impatiently for their gazes to meet, and when they did he found it hard to disguise the desire he felt. He smiled quickly, hoping she hadn't seen, but he doubted it. Even though he'd known her for less than two days, Jackson knew she was a very perceptive woman.

He stood and held the back of the vacant chair next to him. 'Here, have a seat. You must be exhausted.'

'Thank you.'

'How did the operation go?' Kyle asked from across the round table.

'Routine,' Susie replied.

'Jackson said you'd been called to Theatre. So it was nothing interesting?'

'Not really. Dislocated shoulder, fractured ulna, radius and Colles'.'

'Sports injury?' Kyle teased.

'No,' she replied with a laugh. 'Actually, the patient sustained a fall.'

'Do you have something against sports injuries?' Jackson asked with professional curiosity.

'Yes. A good percentage of the injuries I treat have been sustained when people have been playing sport.' She noticed a few nods around the table. 'I'm not denying that playing sport is a fun and healthy way to keep fit, but most people are often careless whilst they're doing it. A bit of forethought, in a lot of instances, would go a long way to preventing many of the injuries I see.'

'I completely agree,' another woman said. She was a physiotherapist and added her thoughts to the conversation. Jackson motioned to the waiter who nodded in understanding and soon brought out a meal for Susie.

'Thank you,' she said with surprise. Jackson's thoughtfulness touched her deeply. How was she supposed to resist him when he did such nice things? 'I thought I might have missed out.'

'I knew you'd be hungry,' he told her softly, delighted that he'd impressed her. He felt himself preen like a peacock and couldn't stop it.

'After all, you've been going non-stop since lunchtime.'

'I'm famished,' she agreed, and tucked right in. He was pleased to see she had a healthy appetite and didn't appear concerned about her figure. Alison had been the same. In fact, Susie had many of the same qualities as Alison and in a strange way it comforted him. Perhaps that was the reason he'd been drawn to Susie in the first place.

As far as looks went, they were like chalk and cheese. Alison had been a bit shorter than Susie, who he guessed to be about five feet, eight inches. Where Susie had long auburn hair, Alison's had been blonde and short. Susie had blue eyes, Alison's had been brown.

Yet a lot of their mannerisms were very similar. The way they walked. The intelligence that was reflected in their eyes and the way they could both make him laugh. It was uncanny and nerve-racking at the same time. He enjoyed the intellectual stimulation but he wasn't the type of man to have casual relationships, and as he was only here until the end of the week, it would be unfair to both of them.

However, it stood to reason that he'd be attracted to a woman with similar qualities, but where his feelings for Alison had grown over time, his immediate awareness of Susie had caught him completely off guard.

Alison had remained working as his secretary after they'd married and had supported him wholeheartedly in his career, but he hadn't been able to discuss his patients with her. Or get her opinion on an operating technique. Or—he glanced at Susie—stand across an operating table and work methodically with her as though they'd worked together their entire lives.

He had family and friends in Melbourne, waiting for him to finish this tour. He had a house, a car…a life. A life without Alison. The memories of Alison, which had overpowered him before he'd left, made Jackson frown. There was still so much he had to work through.

'Are you all right?' Susie's soft words cut into his thoughts and he quickly turned to look at her, the frown disappearing.

'Yes.'

Susie smiled at him. 'You were concentrating so hard on your empty plate that I thought you might be performing a secret male bonding ritual with it.'

Jackson chuckled, feeling instantly better. 'Close, but no cigar.'

'My dad used to get far-off looks in his eyes sometimes after dinner. Once, when I was seventeen, I asked him what he was thinking about. He said he was reflecting on life.'

'Good answer.'

'He said with ten children he hardly ever had a moment to himself, and when he finally *did* get a moment, he'd remember the good things that had happened. Like when he and my mother got married. The birth of each of his children. Stuff like that.'

'He sounds like a nice man.'

Susie nodded. 'Yeah, he is.'

'Do they live far from you?'

'No. About an hour's drive north from Brisbane.'

'On the Sunshine Coast?'

'That's right. Oh, no. I forgot,' Susie gasped and bit her lower lip.

'Problem?'

'I forgot to ask you. Do you know of a general surgeon called Nicholas Sterling?'

'The name's familiar.' Jackson thought. 'Didn't he do a visiting professorship quite a few years ago?'

'About nine years ago, yes. Well, he and his wife live on the Sunshine Coast and were hoping to get to Brisbane to hear you speak. Unfortunately, they're completely swamped and are unable to come down, so they wondered if you'd like to come up and visit them? With you mentioning the Sunshine Coast, it jogged my memory.'

'I'd be delighted to catch up with them but the only time I have free is Thursday evening and Saturday.'

'I know. I told Mallory that Saturday would probably be the best. You could hire a car and drive up, meet them and get back in time for your flight out.'

'Why don't you come, too?' He watched the way her eyes widened at his suggestion. 'That way, you can catch up with your friends and I won't have to worry about getting lost or taking the wrong turn.'

'Uh…well, I hadn't planned on going.'

'Neither had I,' he replied. 'You're not on call, are you?'

'No.'

'There we go, then. It's all settled. I'll pay all petrol and travelling costs if you provide the car.'

Susie found herself nodding, wondering how on earth that had happened so quickly. One minute she was telling him about it and the next she was the chauffeur.

'Now all I have to do is break the news to Richard.'

Susie couldn't help but smile at his wry grin. She knew he was only joking and that Richard would do whatever Jackson said. She'd observed him to be fair and understanding when he dealt with his staff but at the end of the day it was his word and his alone that they all followed. If he really didn't want to do something, he didn't do it.

Susie managed to get through the rest of dinner, her head still reeling with the fact that she'd be alone with Jackson in her car. What would they talk about? They'd be sitting so close. It would be a very intimate situation and the thought thrilled and scared her at the same time.

That was Saturday. A lot of things could happen before then. Perhaps Nick and Mallory might have simultaneous cancellations and be able to get down to Brisbane after all. Perhaps Richard might insist on accompanying them. Perhaps she might be called away to an emergency. There was no point dwelling on it so

Susie forced herself to put it right out of her mind, knowing she'd be thinking about it again before the evening was out.

Susie's mobile phone rang, bringing her back to reality. She quickly answered it, frowning as she listened to the information. 'I'll be right there,' she replied.

'You don't seem to be able to get through a complete dinner. It's either the beginning or the end,' Jackson jested.

'Anything wrong, Susie?' Kyle asked.

'Not really. They want to transfer a patient out of the hospital.'

'Now?' Kyle glanced at his watch. 'It's almost midnight.'

'Makes sense,' Jackson replied with a nod. 'So they want you to check he's all right to be moved.'

'Yes.'

'Who's the patient?' Kyle asked, completely baffled.

'Blade Fargo,' Susie replied as she stood and collected her bag.

'Blade Fargo! You operated on Blade Fargo and you didn't tell me!' Kyle asked incredulously.

'Oh, not you, too.' Susie laughed. 'Perhaps it's just as well you weren't in Theatre, Kyle.

We had enough trouble with the theatre nurses drooling over him. I'd better get going. Goodnight,' she said, her gaze encompassing the table in general.

'I'll walk you out,' Jackson offered.

'It's all right, Jackson,' Kyle said quickly gulping his coffee and standing. 'I'll go with her. I'm not going to miss the opportunity of meeting one of my favourite movie stars.'

Susie met Jackson's gaze, a small smile on her lips. He returned it. 'See you tomorrow, then.'

'Sure. Will you be there for ward round? I'm just asking,' she hurried on, a teasing glint in her eyes, 'so I know not to start without you.'

Jackson laughed. 'Oh, you're funny. I don't think we're scheduled for ward round but if there's a change, we'll let you know.'

'Just so long as you do it before eight-thirty, otherwise you'll have to join in whenever you get there.'

A few of the other people at their table laughed, knowing what had happened that morning.

'We'll do our best,' Jackson remarked, and held out his hand to Susie. Deprived of spending a few minutes alone with her, he felt the need to touch her at least. Susie slowly slid her hand into his and held it firmly. Her skin was soft and smooth and Jackson couldn't resist stroking it gently with his thumb.

His gaze met hers and held for a split second. He saw a flash of longing enter her blue depths and felt a stirring deep within. Conscious of the people around them, he reluctantly let go of her hand. 'I hope you won't be held up too long at the hospital.'

'You and me both,' she replied, and he delighted that her tone was a little unsteady.

'Ready, Susie?' Kyle asked, eager to leave.

Susie turned from Jackson, cleared her throat and nodded at her registrar. As they walked out, Kyle mumbled, 'I still can't believe you didn't call me to assist you. Blade Fargo!'

'Jackson was there.'

'Jackson assisted you?'

'Yes. Problem?'

'No.' Kyle frowned as they waited for the lift. 'It's just that he's so…well…qualified and there he was, assisting you.'

'Oh, so I'm not qualified?'

'Come on, Susie. You know what I mean.'

'I do, Kyle. Jackson wanted to assist. Think about it. The last time he would have helped out in an emergency situation would have been before he started the VOP.'

'I guess so. A bit of variety is good for the soul.'

Susie chuckled. 'Something like that.' As they rode the lift down to the ground floor and waited for the valet to retrieve her car, Susie wondered whether Jackson felt like that in his private life. Perhaps, since his wife's death, he preferred variety. Perhaps he was the type of man to have a woman in every port—or, rather, hospital he visited.

Even as the thought presented itself, she rejected it. He didn't seem the type. Then again, she'd seriously misjudged both Walter and Greg. Could she really trust her instincts as far as Jackson was concerned?

When they arrived at the hospital, it was to find Blade's manager, Margo, in a complete tizz. 'Finally! You're here. We need to move him *now*,' she stormed. 'The fans have all gone home and if we don't do it soon, they'll be back and annoying him again.'

'Isn't that the price of fame?' Susie commented as she started her examination. Kyle, who she'd thought might turn into a groupie, was the consummate professional.

'You're showing no signs of any complications,' she told Blade. 'But it's still too early to tell. Where did you say you'd be going?'

'To a hotel,' Margo answered for him. 'He'll have a private doctor and private nurses to take care of him. So, please, save us all some time and sign him over or he'll just discharge himself.'

Susie clenched her teeth but forced a smile. 'I'll need to talk to the doctor who'll be taking over his treatment,' she said. 'And the nursing staff.'

'Well, we haven't actually employed anyone yet. We just need to get him moved!' Margo huffed, before flipping open her bag and taking out a cigarette. Susie watched her in disbelief.

'Margo,' Blade said tiredly, 'put that away. This is a hospital.'

'What? Oh.' Margo looked at the cigarette in her hand as though she had no idea where it had come from. 'Sorry,' she replied, and Susie realised the other woman simply ran on nerves.

'Listen, why don't we sit down and discuss the best course of action for Blade? He needs to be monitored for the next twenty-four hours at least. I think I might be able to help out in recommending a nurse to help you. As far as a doctor goes, how about either Kyle here or I do house calls twice a day? It would only be for the next few days and after that you'll be fine with weekly or fortnightly check-ups.'

Blade nodded. 'Sounds fair. What do you think, Margo?'

'As long as it means we can move you now, I don't care.'

'Which hotel will you be staying at?' Susie asked, and wasn't surprised when he named the hotel where Jackson was staying. After all, it was Brisbane's finest.

'Hey,' Kyle remarked. 'We've just come from there. We had dinner there this evening. Food was fantastic.'

'Good to hear.' Blade sighed and closed his eyes. Susie realised he was exhausted—and rightly so.

'Do you have transport organised?'

'It's all ready to go,' Margo replied, her impatience returning. 'So, can we move him *now*?'

'Let me arrange the nurse first,' Susie replied, and headed to the nurses' station to use the phone. She motioned for Kyle to follow her. 'I'd like you to monitor him tonight. Is that all right with you?'

'Sure. Wow! I get to be orthopaedic doctor to Blade Fargo.'

Susie smiled. 'Quite a feather in your cap, eh?'

'I'll just head over to the residence where I keep a change of clothes and meet you back here,' he said, already starting out the door.

Susie sat down and called Switchboard. After obtaining Patti's home number, she gave her a call.

'Hi, Patti. Sorry to wake you,' Susie said.

'I'm not on call,' Patti told her with a yawn. 'I don't even work there now. Remember?'

'I know, which is why I called. I have an…unusual request to make of you.'

'Hmm?'

'Blade Fargo. How would you like to nurse him privately for the next few days?' There was silence on the end of the phone. 'Patti?'

'Did I hear you right? No. I must still be asleep and this is a dream.'

Susie laughed. 'You heard me right, Patti. His manager wants him out of the hospital— it's a security risk.' Susie gave Patti the details of where he was staying. 'We'll be moving him there within the hour. Kyle will be there as well—just for tonight.'

'Is he showing any sign of complications?'

'Not yet but I only operated on him about five hours ago.'

'Too soon to tell,' Patti mumbled.

'So will you do it?'

'You'd better believe it,' the nurse replied with a laugh.

'Good. We can organise the paperwork with the agency tomorrow, if that's all right.'

'I'll take care of it.'

'OK. I'll see you at the hotel, then.' Susie relayed the good news to Margo as Blade was now sleeping. The manager sprang into action, pulling out her mobile phone which Susie quickly took off her. 'Your phone should be switched off,' she said, and pointed to several posters on the walls, telling people to turn their phones off. 'If you need to make some calls, please, feel free to use the pay phones,' she continued, and led the way.

Finally, everything was organised and Kyle travelled with them in the back of the limousine. Blade was collected from one of the back entrances to the hospital after a security sweep by his bodyguards had revealed no movie fans to be found. Susie followed them in her car and greeted the valet attendant with a tired smile. 'I won't be too long,' she told him.

As she was waiting for the lifts, Patti came up beside her. 'Oh, good,' Susie said. 'Thanks for doing this at such short notice.'

'Are you kidding?' the nurse asked. 'This is just the best thing that's ever happened to me. So where is he?'

'Being brought in through the back entrance.' They took the lift up to the fourth floor, where a number of suites were located. Margo had told her the room number but as there were bodyguards standing guard in the corridor, Susie surmised that they'd beaten Blade there.

A door marked STAFF ONLY opened and Blade was brought through in a wheelchair. He was just being taken into the room when a door along the corridor opened. Susie looked around and saw Jackson, dressed in faded denim jeans, a white T-shirt and with damp hair, come through the door.

He stopped when he saw her. 'Susie!' he said in surprise.

'Jackson!' Her surprise equalled his. Her gaze drank in the sight of him dressed in casual clothes, and she could have sworn her heart started having palpitations.

Jackson slowly took a few steps towards her but one of Blade's bodyguards intercepted him. 'No. It's all right,' she said quickly, and held up her hand to stop him. 'He's a colleague of mine.'

'Ma'am, security has to be kept tight,' the bodyguard replied.

'No. You don't understand. This doctor assisted with Mr Fargo's surgery earlier this evening.'

Margo came out of the suite. 'What's going on?' she asked, and then spotted Jackson. 'Oh, hi, again,' she said. 'It's all right.' Her last comments were directed to the bodyguard. 'Has that other equipment come up yet?'

The STAFF ONLY door opened as she spoke and the equipment, which had been hired from a private hospital Susie used to work at, was wheeled through. 'This way,' Margo instructed. The bodyguard followed her and waited for Susie.

'Uh…I'll be there in a moment. Tell Kyle to get things started,' she ordered, and the bodyguard shut the door behind him.

'Doing a little private consulting?' Jackson asked, his tone husky. He didn't move. They simply stood there, staring at each other. Susie's gaze went over him again and she realised his feet were bare. He looked so…different out of his suit. Relaxed. Gorgeous. Sexy!

CHAPTER SIX

Susie tried to swallow but found her throat completely dry. 'Um...I...um, hope the, um...' She trailed off as Jackson took a small step towards her. Her breathing increased and she parted her lips to allow the air to escape more easily, her gaze never leaving his.

Again he moved, slowly closing the distance between them. Susie took an involuntary step backwards, only to encounter the wall. He was like a lion, stalking his prey, slowly... cautiously. She couldn't move, even if she'd wanted to. She was mesmerised by him.

With a few more steps he was standing before her. In her high-heeled shoes, their gazes were almost level. Her gaze flicked to his lips and saw them part.

'Oh,' she gasped, as he raised his hands and placed them on the wall on either side of her head. Her breathing was now so utterly out of control there was no hiding just how much this man affected her. She'd been attracted to other men in the past but never had it been this intense.

She looked up into his eyes, noting the mounting desire there as Jackson slowly leaned closer. His clean, fresh scent only heightened her awareness of him.

'You were saying?' His deep voice washed over her and Susie's eyelids fluttered closed, savouring the moment. She opened them again and looked longingly at his lips.

'Huh?'

'Didn't you want to...ask me something?'

Did she? She had no idea. Her brain failed her, her only conscious thought being that if Jackson *didn't* kiss her, she'd go insane. The effect he had on her senses was sending them spiralling out of control. Her body was in tune with his as she silently urged him to come even closer.

How much longer was he going to torture them? If she could get her arms to move, she'd reach out and bring his lips to hers. She was paralysed, no, hypnotised, and there was nothing she could do about it, such was the effect Jackson had on her.

'Captivating,' he whispered. Never before had he felt like this. It *had* to be right—but even if it was wrong, there was no denying that the only thing he wanted to do right at this very second was to claim Susie's luscious lips in a mind-shattering kiss. A kiss that would satisfy them both—of that he was absolutely sure.

Closer and closer he came until his breath was mixing with hers. Susie closed her eyes, unable to summon the strength to keep them open. She waited, waited impatiently for his mouth to touch hers while still enjoying the sensations he was evoking throughout her body.

The click of a door being opened, together with Kyle's voice saying 'I'll check with Susie', penetrated the sensual haze with a jolt.

Susie's eyes snapped open, her limbs came to life and she quickly ducked under Jackson's arm, trying to compose herself. Her legs were like jelly and as she took a step away she stumbled.

'Hey, Susie,' Kyle said as he spotted her and then quickly held out a steadying hand. 'You all right?'

Not trusting herself to speak, she nodded.

'Jackson?' Kyle looked past her and Susie risked a glance over her shoulder. He was casually leaning against the wall, his hands in his jeans pockets.

'Kyle.'

'Are you staying on this floor?'

'Yes, a few doors down.' He kept his gaze away from Susie's, although the way she'd looked a few seconds ago would now be burned in his memory for ever. Her face had been turned expectantly up towards his, her lips parted, her eyes closed, her skin tinged with a faint pink glow. Beautiful! 'I hear Blade Fargo is one of my neighbours.' He forced himself to ease away from the wall.

He was determined to ensure that Kyle didn't pick up on the sexual tension that existed between Susie and himself. He needed to protect her as best he could, and if that mean not looking at her then he wouldn't.

'Yeah, and Susie and I are his doctors.' Kyle said excitedly. 'Come and say g'day,' he urged, and knocked on the closed hotel door. It was opened by one of the bodyguards and Kyle headed in.

Susie hung back, anxious for a look, a word—*something*—from Jackson to reassure her. Instead, he gave her a wide berth and for the first time since she'd met him he went through the door before her.

She was hurt. Didn't he realise she needed some reassurance? Had Kyle not interrupted them, Jackson would have kissed her and there was no way she would have resisted. She'd wanted it just as desperately as he had.

Feeling suddenly cold and bereft, Susie rubbed her arms as the first spark of anger ignited deep inside. She followed him into the room. How dared he pretend nothing had happened? Although, she realised, nothing *had* happened and perhaps that was why she was starting to feel so utterly frustrated.

How dared she allow him to have the ability to affect her in such a way? Her anger grew and it encompassed herself as well as Jackson. She'd promised herself *not* to allow men to affect her like this yet here she was, frustrated and cross because of Jackson.

Perhaps she should thank Kyle for interrupting them. Perhaps she should consider this a lucky escape. After all, if they *had* kissed, she would have had more physical sensations to fight. Perhaps she was better off.

'Would that be right, Susie?' Kyle was asking her, and she realised that everyone in the room was looking at her expectantly—except Jackson.

'Uh…well…um…' she spluttered, not at all sure what Kyle had asked her.

'I think you're spot on, Kyle,' Jackson answered. 'Good work.'

'Ah... Absolutely,' Susie responded, finally finding her voice. Her hostility towards Jackson diminished a bit as she acknowledged that he'd just rescued her. She needed to get out of there, to sort out her emotions before she made a fool of herself. 'If that's all you need...' she glanced at Blade and then at Kyle, her gaze avoiding Jackson's '...I think I'll head home. It's been a very hectic day and tomorrow promises to be no less. Call me if you need me,' she told Kyle as she turned and headed to the door.

'I'd better be going, too,' Jackson announced to the room.

'Aw, come on,' Margo purred, and Susie watched as the other woman crossed to Jackson's side and linked her arm with his. 'Surely you don't have to go *just* yet? Now that we've got Blade settled, we can all relax.'

Susie groaned inwardly and continued out of the door, which one of the bodyguards held open for her. 'Stay and relax,' she muttered as she stormed over to the lifts. 'That man doesn't know his own charm and probably has every woman he meets falling in love with him.' She assaulted the down button, pressing it repeatedly.

'Mumbling to yourself?' Jackson asked. She didn't turn around. Instead, she pressed the down button again.

'I'll walk you out.'

'There's no need,' she replied between clenched teeth.

Jackson watched as she pressed the button again, muttering something about slow hotel lifts. He frowned, unsure why she was so angry. 'It's no trouble,' he told her.

Susie met his gaze. 'I don't care if it's an imposition to you or not, the fact is that I don't want you to walk me out. I'm a big girl, Jackson, and I'm more than capable of getting into the lift, walking to the valet desk and waiting for my car.' She pressed the button yet again. 'That's if this lift ever gets here.'

'You're angry with me,' he stated in surprise. 'Why?'

'Oh, that's right. As far as you're concerned, you've not done anything wrong.' Her temper was at boiling point. She was cross with him, cross with herself and cross with the lift. She glanced around for an exit sign and stormed over to the door marked STAIRS.

'Susie!' Jackson charged after her, completely baffled as to why she was upset. The concrete stairs were cold beneath his feet but that was the least of his worries. 'Talk to me,' he demanded, his voice echoing. The clip-clop of Susie's shoes reverberated around the stairwell and he was pleased to note she was holding onto the railing. She'd already stumbled once tonight and, as he'd realised the previous evening, she wasn't at all comfortable in heels higher than an inch.

'There's nothing to say.' She rounded the bend and started on the next flight. She was grateful that Blade's suite hadn't been on the twentieth floor but, given the way she was feeling, she wouldn't have cared how many flights of stairs she had to walk down. All she wanted was to get out of the hotel and away from Jackson.

'Nothing to say? You're being stubborn and irrational.'

Susie stopped and whirled around to look up at him. He stopped, too. 'Stubborn? Irrational?'

'Yes.' There were only two steps between them and Jackson slowly moved down one, hoping she wouldn't move. It didn't work.

She whirled around again and started clopping her way down the noisy stairwell. 'So what if I *am* being irrational? I've got good reason.'

'Then tell me what it is,' he said, starting to get a bit fed up with the situation himself. He took the stairs two at a time, passing her. He barred her way just before she reached the door that led to the lobby.

'Look, if I've done something wrong, at least tell me about it so I can apologise.'

Susie gazed at him and felt her anger begin to dissipate. She sighed. 'It's the fact that you don't know you've done anything wrong that's made me angry.' That and her own uncontrollable reaction to him. She had to become stronger. She had to fight the attraction between them with every ounce of strength she had.

'Wanting to kiss you was wrong?' If there was one thing he'd learnt from his marriage, it was that communication was paramount. Then again, Alison had always been willing to talk things through and eventually come to see things his way. Whereas Susie seemed to be as stubborn as a mule.

'Oh, you know it was,' she said, her anger returning. 'I hardly know you, Jackson. You might have a girl in every…hospital,' she spluttered. She saw his jaw clench and his eyes darken. 'You've been travelling for so long, you're bound to get…well…lonely and—'

'So you just think I kiss any woman who shows an interest in me, eh?'

'How do I know? You might.' The last thing Susie wanted to think about now was Jackson kissing other women. Jealousy reared its ugly head.

'Even though we've spent such a short time together, Susie, I thought the answer to that question might have been obvious. For all I know, you might be the type of woman who gives in to every guy who makes a pass at you.'

'What? How dare you?'

'Ah, so you don't like it either. It's all right for you to accuse me of bad behaviour but not vice versa.'

He had a point. Susie looked down at the stairs, trying to control her emotions and her thoughts. Finally, she raised her head to look into his eyes, eyes that had the ability to make her forget all rational thought. 'Look, all I was saying is that you're a very handsome man and I'm sure you've met plenty of women during the VOP who would have been more than willing to indulge in a brief affair while you were in town.'

'And what if there were?'

Susie's eyes widened in surprise. Was he admitting to it? Was he a womaniser? 'Were there?' she asked quietly, trying hard to control her disappointment.

'Yes.'

She felt as though he'd hit her. Her mouth opened in disbelief. She'd been hoping against hope that he wasn't that way and now he was admitting as much.

'Yes, there have been women who've made passes at me during the VOP—*but* I didn't take any of them up on their offers. Susie, I've been working through a lot of emotions during this tour and the last thing I needed was…entanglements.' He held out his hand to her. 'Until you.' His tone was soft and endearing, urging her to trust him.

She looked at his hand but didn't take it. He dropped it back to his side and nodded. 'You're the first woman I've *wanted* to kiss since Alison's death. Is it so wrong that I'd follow through on that instinct?'

'You shouldn't have.' Susie shook her head for emphasis, her determination returning.

'Why not?' His tone held a hint of impatience.

'Because it just complicates things even more.' She sidestepped him and stalked through the door, into the lobby.

'As I recall,' he said as he went after her, 'you were quite willing for it to happen.'

Susie stopped and turned to face him glad that, except for the bare minimum of staff, the lobby was deserted. 'I am not having this discussion with you *here*.'

'Then come back up to my room and we'll discuss it there.'

'Ha. Come back to your room? That would be the *last* thing I do.'

'Why?'

Susie opened her mouth to speak but couldn't. She wanted to tell him that if she went up to his room there was no way she'd be able to resist him. He would kiss her and she would willingly let him. She knew it was because she wanted it, more than she wanted anything else right now, but she'd also given in to her wants before and it had ended in heartbreak.

'I'll tell you why,' he continued. 'You don't want to come back to my room because you can't trust yourself.' He lowered his voice and took a step closer. As he did, he stubbed his toe on a nearby table and grunted in pain.

Susie reached out and steadied the vase of flowers on the table before glancing down at his foot. He'd flexed his ankle to hold the toes upwards and was hobbling towards a chair. She looked into his eyes and saw the pain there.

'Let me look at it,' she said, and reached for his foot.

'No. It's fine. I can take care of it.'

'Stop being such a martyr and let me look at it.' Susie grabbed his heel and lifted it up.

'Is everything all right?' one of the staff asked.

'It's *fine*.' Jackson glared at Susie as she tweaked his sore toe.

'Sorry.' She grinned at him and continued checking the range of motion. 'Not broken,' she announced, and turned to face the staff member. 'He'll be fine,' she said. 'My prescription is two paracetamol and bed rest. Perhaps you might help Professor Myers back up to his room.' Susie smiled sweetly, enjoying Jackson's disadvantage.

'I'm fine,' he repeated, and stood to prove it.

'Well, if that will be all, I'll be on my way.' Susie handed the staff member her valet ticket, and after a brief nod he left them. 'No charge for the examination,' she told Jackson.

'How generous of you.' He frowned and she realised that she'd better not try to push him any further as his mood had changed drastically. Previously he'd been willing to reason, to calmly discuss things. Now he wasn't in such a good mood and she didn't blame him—stubbed toes were painful.

Susie decided to take pity on him. 'Go and rest. I'll see you tomorrow,' she said, and turned away from him. It was either that or throw herself into his arms. He looked so gorgeous, standing there in his faded denims, his blue eyes filled with exhaustion. It had been hard to resist but with every step she took away from him she grew more proud of her success.

'Susie,' he called softly, and she turned around, gazing at him expectantly.

'Thanks.'

'For what?'

'For talking to me.'

Was he trying to make her feel guilty? Both Greg and Walter had used that tactic and she'd

fallen for it every time. His next words, however, made her rethink his sentiments.

'I know it wasn't easy for you.' His gaze
bored into hers and she felt that familiar stirring sensation in her stomach. 'Drive carefully.' With that, he turned and hobbled over
to the lift. Susie watched him, torn between
amusement at the sight he made and the urge
to assist him.

'Your car is here, ma'am.'

Susie forced herself to look away and
walked out of the hotel. Jackson pressed the
button for the lift and watched her go. She was
magnificent and she had become far too important to him far too quickly.

The lift bell chimed and Jackson hobbled in,
recalling the way he'd felt as she'd cradled his
foot in her hand. As she'd been angry with
him, he'd half expected her to be rough with
her examination but instead she'd been extremely gentle. Her skin had been soft against
his, and although she'd touched him in a professional, medical way, he hadn't been able to
stop the stirring of excitement that had shot
through him.

At the fourth floor, he walked to his door
and reached into his back pocket for the key-
card. Once inside, he opened the curtains and

turned off the lights before settling back on the bed, propping his foot up on a few pillows.

He'd come so close to kissing her—so agonisingly close. Ever since they'd met, Jackson had wanted to sample her mouth, and the longer he waited, the more urgent the desire grew.

He knew the score. He knew she didn't want to get hurt and he had no desire to hurt her. He raked an unsteady hand though his hair and groaned in confusion. What about Alison? Would she mind if he kissed another woman? The feelings of betrayal hit him forcefully but it still didn't stop him from making a decision. He'd be leaving at the end of the week and, regardless of the war taking place inside him, he knew one thing for sure.

Despite everything, he *needed* to kiss Susie.

Susie didn't sleep at all well that night and when she did manage to drift off sometime before dawn, she dreamt she was anxiously trying to glue a vase back together. The pieces were tiny and the tears she was crying kept blurring her vision. She stood and looked down at the mess and only then did she realise that the vase was heart-shaped.

The realisation only increased the urgency as she was expecting a new delivery of flowers at any minute. Working frantically, Susie managed to piece the heart-shaped vase back together. The doorbell rang and she hurried to answer it. There stood Jackson, holding a bunch of roses. Susie stared aghast at the vase. She couldn't accept the flowers from Jackson because the vase was still drying.

She *wanted* the flowers but where was she going to put them? Anxiousness and fear gripped Susie's heart as Jackson held the flowers out to her. What was she going to do? What was she going to do?

She woke suddenly, her heart pounding fiercely against her ribs. 'Just a dream,' she whispered to herself. She lay back and sighed, breathing deeply. She glanced at the clock and realised it was one minute before her alarm was due to go off. 'So much for a good night's sleep,' she muttered, and clambered out of bed.

She glanced at herself in the mirror. She looked horrible. 'Perhaps a little make-up might be in order today.' Susie finished getting dressed, deciding that she wouldn't chance breakfast as her stomach didn't feel settled.

She arrived at the hospital and went straight to the ward. All through the round, she kept anxiously glancing at the door in case Jackson decided to join them again. He didn't. Feeling a bit flat, she returned to her office, hoping to catch up on paperwork before her theatre list began in half an hour.

Sitting at her desk, it wasn't long before further thoughts of Jackson intruded. Instead of fighting them, she gave in. She was exhausted from fighting her emotions, as well as from lack of sleep. She thought about her dream, reflecting on the symbolism of the heart-shaped vase. It was true that both Walter and Greg had broken her heart and she'd managed to mend it both times.

With Jackson, her feelings for him were so out of proportion to what she'd felt for her fiancés that it was scaring her. She acknowledged that Jackson had more power to hurt her than any other man and that was only after two days of his acquaintance. What would happen if he was around permanently?

'Finished with that file yet?' Todd asked as he walked into her office.

'Huh? Oh, sorry.' She looked down at the open file and realised that she hadn't started. So much for getting through her paperwork. 'Not yet.'

'Everything all right?' he asked.

'Yes.'

'Sure? You seem to be…preoccupied.'

She shrugged and looked down at her work, not wanting him to see the tell-tale blush she could feel creeping into her cheeks. 'It's been a busy two days,' she rationalised.

'It certainly has. Today, thankfully, isn't going to be as hectic.' Todd went over her schedule, which included her operating list that morning and time to work on her research proposal in the afternoon. 'Then there's a dinner this evening.'

Susie groaned. 'I don't think my feet will be able to handle it.'

Todd laughed. 'You've been doing a great job walking in those ridiculously high heels.'

'Hmm. Well, I think I might wear a trouser suit tonight so I can keep the heels low.'

'You can't do that!'

'Why not?' She narrowed her gaze, noticing the teasing twinkle in his eyes.

'We've all been enjoying the transformation.'

'What are you talking about?' Had people noticed the chemistry between her and Jackson? Susie's spine stiffened as panic started to grip her.

'Well, it's the first time people have seen you more formally dressed. Usually, it's just one suit after another, but the other night you looked *hot* in that black dress.'

Susie sighed with relief and relaxed into her chair. Her clothes. Todd had been referring to her clothes. 'Hot, eh? Actually, I was neither hot nor cold,' she told him, her humour returning.

Todd laughed. 'You know what I meant.'

The phone on her desk shrilled to life and she instantly hoped it was Jackson. In the next instant, she dreaded it being Jackson. Oh, would she ever get control of her wayward emotions again? She reached out for the receiver but Todd beat her to it. 'Dr Monahan's office.'

He stared at her, making her feel uneasy again. 'I'll put you through.' He put the caller on hold and handed the receiver to Susie. 'It's A and E.'

'Oh.' Why did she feel so deflated? Surely it was a good thing that Jackson hadn't been calling her, especially after what had transpired last night. She took the receiver from Todd. 'Do you need me for anything else?' she asked, and he shook his head.

As she took the call, Todd left her office, giving her some privacy. 'Dr Monahan,' she said, and listened to the triage sister.

'Susie, I've been paging you for the last fifteen minutes.'

'You have?' Susie clipped her pager off her waistband and stared at it. 'Uh—sorry. Battery is flat. Is there a problem?'

'I know you're not on call but a patient came in about half an hour ago with a mangled hand.'

'Oh?' Susie's interest was immediate. The research proposal she was in the process of drawing up was a continuation of her previous research concerning microsurgery of the hand. 'Can I come and take a look?'

'That's the reason I'm calling. She's been seen by Mr Petunia but he asked me to call and let you know. He thought it might be good for your research.'

'He's right. I'll come down now before Theatre and take a look.'

Susie quickly changed the battery in her pager before heading to A and E. She found Mr Petunia and together they discussed the patient.

'Her name is Hilda Kazinski, a forty-seven-year-old factory worker. She got her hand caught in a conveyor belt.'

'Ooh.' Susie winced. 'Has she had X-rays?'

'She's in Radiology now, but from what I can see the phalanges are a mess with bad metacarpal damage. I think it best if I give her over into your care and then you can request whatever other scans you need.'

'Great. Thanks.' Susie shook hands with her colleague and headed off to Radiology in search of her new patient. Hilda Kazinski was having the last X-ray taken when Susie arrived. She introduced herself and told Hilda about the transfer of care.

'Why?' Hilda asked, her words slurring a bit from the pain relief she'd been given.

'Well, upper-limb injuries and in particular hand reconstruction are a speciality of mine.'

'But I don't have private health cover,' her patient protested.

'That's fine. You'll still be under the public system but I'll be treating you.'

'Because I have a bad hand injury.'

'Yes. I've done extensive research in this field and am qualified to perform the surgery you'll require.'

'So you're the best, eh?'

Susie smiled. 'In a manner of speaking, yes. Listen, you just rest here while I go and check on the status of your X-rays.' Susie headed off to find the radiologist, leaving Hilda in the care of the A and E nurses.

'Do you require any other views, Susie?' the radiologist asked as he continued to report on them.

'No. These look fine. She'll need an MRI and a CT scan, but for the moment these look great.' Susie studied the illuminated images before her one more time before turning away. 'I'll get the other scans organised and then I'm due in Theatre.'

Susie managed to get everything done before she headed up to the elective theatres for her list. Everything progressed smoothly and she degowned just after one o'clock, pleased with what she could accomplish when she pushed thoughts of Jackson aside.

With determination in her step, she headed back to A and E to find out where Hilda was and to get things ready for surgery. Hilda was back from MRI and sleeping. Susie sat down in the tearoom to examine the films, quickly eating her lunch as she did so. She heard the door open and close again but didn't look up as she was too engrossed in the scans.

'Interesting case?'

A flood of excitement washed over her at the sound of Jackson's voice. She looked up in surprise, right into his deep blue eyes. Eyes that had plagued her dreams, intruded during her day and were now gazing at her with repressed emotion. She breathed in and swallowed at the same time, choking on the last mouthful of her sandwich. She coughed violently and Jackson patted her on the back.

'Take it easy,' he said, before quickly fetching a glass of water.

'I'm fine,' she whispered, but then coughed again, proving herself wrong.

'You seem to be forever choking,' he jested.

'Only when you're around,' she mumbled as she took a sip. She cleared her throat. 'What brings you to the hospital?' His spicy aftershave entwined itself about her and she fought hard to resist it.

'Aren't I allowed to call in without an invitation?' He smiled as he leaned against the edge of the table. His firm thigh was so close to her arm that she could feel the heat radiating from him. Her breath caught in her throat and her mouth went dry.

Susie took another sip of the water. 'No…it's just that…I thought you were lecturing.'

'I was.' He picked up a scan and held it to the light. 'Ouch.' He frowned. 'Horrible injury.'

'She caught her hand in a conveyor belt. I want to get to Theatre soon so I can make a start on it.' Why was she so aware of him? It simply wasn't fair! She moved her arm to gather up the films and accidentally brushed against his leg in the process. An explosion similar to fireworks burst throughout her and her eyelids fluttered closed for a brief second. He was silent and she quickly looked up at him. He was gazing down at her with burning desire reflected in his eyes.

Jackson fought hard for control but it wasn't easy. She set him on fire. With the mildest touch, with the merest flutter of her eyes, with the perfume which was driving him insane. She set him on fire and he was sick of dousing the flames.

He fought for something to say. 'Er…how many reconstructions like this have you done before?' He couldn't help the huskiness that accompanied his words, and as Susie looked away from him, he feasted his eyes on the slender, smooth skin of her neck. Her hair was clipped back at her nape and he remembered how incredible it had looked flowing freely around her face last night.

'Um…quite a few.' Susie shifted her chair slightly, trying to put a bit of distance between them without appearing rude.

'Are you operating in the theatre with the viewing gallery?'

'No.'

'Pity.'

'Why?'

'This type of operation should be videoed for future reference.'

'There are already a few in the hospital's library,' she told him as she concentrated hard on putting the films in their packets, noticing that her hands weren't quite steady.

'Ones that you've done?' He could see she was getting ready to take flight and he wanted to stop her. If he edged a little to the side and bent his head, he was positive he'd be able to capture her sweet lips with his. Lips he ached to feel.

'Yes.'

'I'm impressed.'

'Really?' She looked up at him from where she sat, warmed by his praise. Here was a man who had worked with some of the finest surgeons in the world and he was impressed because some of her operations had been recorded on video.

'Yes.' He gazed into her eyes and leaned closer. 'I know only the most impressive surgery is recorded.' Unable to resist touching her any longer, he reached out and tenderly ran his fingers down her cheek, bringing them to rest beneath her chin. 'Susie.' As he breathed her name, he lifted her chin slightly, angling her head towards his.

Susie gazed at him, her heart pounding wildly against her ribs. He was going to kiss her. This time, for sure, he was going to kiss her. She watched beneath her lashes as his head slowly drew closer. She shouldn't be doing this. She had an operation to concentrate on.

'Jackson… I—' She didn't manage to finish her sentence as his mouth finally made contact with hers.

CHAPTER SEVEN

JACKSON groaned as Susie leaned closer to him, showing him that, despite her words, she wanted this as much as he did. Her lips were soft and pliable, just as he'd known they would be.

Susie sighed and opened her mouth beneath his subtle urging, elated to finally give in to her feelings. He tasted like chocolate and coffee—both sweet and addictive. She knew she was going under and there was nothing she could do to stop it.

Without breaking contact, his hands cupped her face, urging her closer, and she edged from her chair, reaching out for him as she moved to stand in front of him. She was amazed to find her usually wobbly legs were willing to support her.

He shifted to accommodate her, his hands sliding around her back as he deepened the kiss. Never in his wildest dreams had he imagined torture could be so agonisingly delightful. She simply melted into his embrace as though they'd been made for each other. The realisation only increased the overpowering emotions that were swamping him.

Fireworks like she'd never felt before exploded one after the other throughout her body, each new burst sending her senses spiralling out of control. This was impossible. Never before had she been so overwhelmed by a kiss. Then again, this wasn't any ordinary kiss. The spark that flowed freely between them now had been repressed for two and a half full days, building and simmering within, only to be unleashed with such intensity it was no wonder it was unique.

Her hands were pressed against his chest and she could feel the contours of his firm, muscled torso beneath his cotton shirt. Delighted at being able to touch him at last, she slid her hands up his chest, entwining them about his neck, her fingers plunging into his rich, dark hair. A low, guttural sound, primitive, came from him and she revelled in her power.

His hands slid ever so slowly down her sides, his fingers splayed outwards, moulding her ribs. His thumbs lightly brushed the underside of her breast and she gasped in shock as yet another wave of pleasure coursed through her.

The power he had over her only ignited his passion even more.

Her excitement was mounting with every passing second and she was having difficulty breathing. What did she care about oxygen when she had Jackson? With a satisfied moan, Susie pulled her mouth from his, dragging air into her lungs, pleased to note that his breathing was just as erratic.

He pressed kisses to her cheek, working his way towards her ear, and she tipped her head to the side, allowing him access. A thousand goose-bumps cascaded over her body, increasing her light-headedness. He was a drug and the more she had of him, the more she knew she'd become addicted.

He brought his hand up and brushed her neck, gently urging her collar aside to make room for his hungry lips. She had the smoothest skin, the most luscious neck, and he doubted whether he'd ever be able to get enough of her. Now that he'd kissed her, the realisation of how incredible they were together only made him want her even more.

He brought his mouth up to meet hers again, their lips mingling together like old friends. Although he wanted nothing more than to deepen the kiss, heighten the intensity, Jackson could feel her starting to withdraw.

He pressed his lips to hers one last time before allowing her to rest her head on his chest, and their breathing slowly returned to normal. His arms embraced her, holding her tightly, never wanting to let her go.

As she stood there, listening to his heart gradually return to a steady rhythm, Susie started to feel uncomfortable and awkward. What would happen now? Jackson had kissed her and it had been...the most powerful experience she'd ever had. Her frazzled mind acknowledged that she would never be the same again. The kisses, the passion, the desire—all of them had changed who she was. Never had she experienced anything like the onslaught of emotions or the intensity of feeling which had just transpired.

His hands rubbed gently up and down her back. She knew it was supposed to relax her but she couldn't stop her body from tensing. What had she done, letting Jackson kiss her? There were several reasons why it had been a bad idea and one of them was that she was due in Theatre.

Reluctantly, he let her go and she took three giant steps backwards. She was having trouble meeting his gaze but eventually her eyes met his.

Helplessness and confusion were running rampant through her mind and along with it came fatigue. She didn't have the energy for a post-mortem on what had just happened and she hoped Jackson realised this. She tucked a stray curl behind her ear and shook her head.

'We shouldn't have done that.' Her words were a whisper.

'Why not?'

'Well, for starters, someone could have walked in and caught us.' She pointed to the door.

'They didn't.' He shrugged nonchalantly.

'I'm due in Theatre soon. I should be concentrating. Hand reconstruction isn't the same as a knee arthroscopy, you know.' She turned and walked over to the sink, bracing her hands on the edge.

'I know the difference,' he replied, and she heard him walk towards her. She was so instinctively aware of him, it frightened her. Jackson rubbed his hands up and down her arms, making her resent her outburst. 'I apologise for the timing. You're right. You should be concentrating.'

He dropped his hands although he didn't move back. Susie felt slightly bereft but drew warmth from the nearness of his body.

'We do, however,' he continued, 'need to talk.'

'No, we don't.' She turned to look at him, determination running through her body. 'We don't need to discuss or dissect what just happened, Jackson. It happened. Let's just leave it at that. Now, if you'll excuse me, I need to get my thoughts in order regarding this operation.' With that, she sidestepped him and walked to the table.

She collected the X-rays and scans, conscious of his gaze upon her. When she reached the door, she congratulated herself on not giving in to the urge to throw herself back into his arms. Just before she opened the door, he spoke.

'We *do* need to talk, Susie, and we will.'

She glanced over her shoulder. Blue eyes which had not too long ago been filled with desire were now filled with determination. Not trusting herself to say anything, she continued out the door, returning to her office with the hope of controlling her trembling body in private.

Jackson stood in the tearoom for a good ten minutes after she'd walked out. His thoughts were completely jumbled and he was having a difficult time making head or tail of them. He'd kissed Susie! He'd kissed another woman! Guilt swamped him and he closed his eyes.

What had he been thinking? He had responsibilities. He had a job to do. His behaviour had been far from professional yet at the same time it was becoming increasingly difficult to control his desire where Susie was concerned.

She was interfering with his work, his concentration, and it wouldn't do. At this moment he was supposed to be working with his staff but he'd needed to see her, needed to touch her, needed to kiss her.

He opened his eyes and paced the room, forcing his thoughts into order. He'd kissed another woman—a woman who wasn't Alison. It had been years since he'd kissed anyone else and now that he had… He shook his head in disgust. What type of man was he? His wife had died only eighteen months ago and here he was yearning for someone else. He was sure if their positions had been reversed, Alison wouldn't have forgotten him so quickly and the knowledge stabbed at his heart.

Jackson grimaced, pushing his fingers roughly through his hair and clenching his jaw. Never before had he allowed any woman to come between him and his work. He'd always separated them into neat little sections. He'd always prided himself on being one hundred per cent focused where work was concerned but now he appeared to have no control whatsoever.

He had responsibilities to the visiting professorship. He had responsibilities to his staff. He had lectures to write, operations to perform and schedule deadlines to meet. Even when the professorship finished in December, he was due back at his hospital in Melbourne. They were waiting for him. He had obligations there as well.

Yet one look at Susie and everything had gone! Gone! He shoved his hands in his pockets, thoroughly disgusted with himself and his behaviour. How could a woman make him lose control—over everything? Everything he'd prided himself on being. Reliable, responsible, respectable.

'Ha!' he snorted in self-disgust. She'd been studying and trying to focus on an extremely difficult procedure and he hadn't cared. Hadn't given her the same consideration he was sure she'd have given him.

He stopped pacing, his jaw clenched tightly. He shouldn't have kissed her. Shouldn't have—but he had. At least he was man enough to accept his actions and take responsibility for them.

Jackson dragged a deep breath into his lungs, the faint traces of her perfume lingering in the air around him. The awareness between them had been almost unbearable yet now *both* knew how incredible they were together. Kissing Susie hadn't solved anything. It had only increased his desire, his yearning, his curiosity—and that made everything worse!

The beeping of his pager was a welcome relief and he stalked across the room to the phone. 'Richard?' he said a moment later.

'Everything is ready for your afternoon lecture,' his aide told him.

'Thanks.'

'Did you manage to get your…business done?'

Jackson heard the slight hint of resentment in Richard's tone. When Jackson had refused to say where he was going or what he would be doing, Richard had started to sulk.

'Yes. I'll meet you in the lecture room.' Jackson replaced the receiver and headed out of the tearoom. At least now he had something else to concentrate on.

Susie was tired of concentrating. It had been a long afternoon in Theatre but at last the first stage of Hilda Kazinski's hand reconstruction was completed. Now they needed to wait and see what happened before she could attempt the next stage.

Wearily she degowned and shuffled to the tearoom to write up the notes. After that task was finished she sat down with a cup of coffee and put her feet up on the seat opposite. Closing her eyes, she sighed, glad the day was coming to an end.

'Ah, they told me you were probably in here.' Todd walked in and sat down. Susie opened one eye to look at him before closing it again. 'You left your pager in Theatre,' he informed her.

Susie smothered a yawn and nodded. 'I'll get it later.'

'How'd the surgery go?'

'Good. We'll see what happens over the next few days.'

'Shall I include her in your research project?'

'I haven't spoken to her about it yet but I'd like her to be part of it.' Susie shrugged. 'There's plenty of time. Right now, my friend, I am going to go home, soak in a tub and crawl into bed.'

'Has the day been that bad?'

Susie's thoughts automatically turned to Jackson and the electrifying kiss they'd shared. Where was he now? What was he thinking? How was she ever going to face him again?

'By the pained expression on your face,' Todd said a moment later, 'it looks as though it's been horrible.'

'No,' she replied quickly. 'No. Not horrible, just…long.'

'Well, I hate to be the bearer of bad news but I've specifically come here to remind you.'

'Of what?'

'You see, I knew you'd forget.'

Susie raised her eyebrows. 'About what?'

'The dinner.'

Susie groaned and slumped forward onto the table, burying her head in her arms. 'No. I'm too tired.' As though to prove her point, she yawned.

Todd only smiled. 'You have to go, Susie.'

'Why?' She buried her head again.

'Because you're the acting head of department. It's your duty to go.' His tone was matter-of-fact. 'Jackson's going to be there,' he said, as though he were dangling a carrot in front of her nose. Susie merely groaned in exasperation. 'Come on,' he said. 'It's almost six-thirty and the dinner starts in an hour.'

'I don't want to go,' she stated stubbornly.

'Drink your coffee, find some energy and put on your happy face.'

'Or?' Again, she looked at him.

'Or I'll quit.'

Susie sat up straight, eyes wide open, body alert. 'You'll what?'

'Ah…knew I could get your attention,' he teased.

'You're mean,' she grumbled, before finishing off her coffee. 'All right. I'll go but only so you don't resign.' She stood and walked to the sink with her empty cup. 'And I want to leave after the main meal.'

'Sure. That's no problem. You don't need to stay until the end but you do need to be there for the beginning.'

'I don't see why,' she mumbled. 'I'm not introducing anyone, I'm not the MC. Hey…'

She looked at him and pointed her finger. 'You're going, aren't you?'

'It's part of my job. Now, go and get changed.' He walked to the door. 'I'll see you there and don't forget to pick up your pager.'

'Yes, boss,' she said, snapping to attention. Todd merely laughed and continued on his way.

Susie did as she was told. She was used to doing as she was told. It probably came from being raised in a houseful of ten children. Someone was always giving her instructions or asking her to do something. Nothing had changed.

'You're thirty-six years old and nothing has changed,' she said out loud as she unlocked the back door of her house. Instead of the relaxing bubble bath, she stepped beneath a hot shower before dressing. Tonight she wore a white embroidered bustier top and a straight, black silk skirt which came to her ankles. As with her other black outfit, there was a split at the back so she could walk without shuffling along like a geisha girl.

She secured her hair up in a high ponytail, letting her curls do their thing. She kept telling herself that she wasn't dressing for Jackson Myers. Oh, sure, he found her attractive—the kiss they'd shared was testimony to it—but she couldn't help thinking that he'd like her hair up like this. Her masses of unruly curls were now out of the way, revealing her long, smooth neck that he'd made much of that afternoon.

The lipstick she chose was one that was guaranteed not to 'kiss off', not that she was planning on doing any kissing tonight. She changed her earrings and decided on impulse not to wear anything around her neck. Just in case.

Oh, who was she kidding? she thought as she slipped her stockinged feet into black shoes and picked up her clutch bag. Of course she was dressing for Jackson. She was eager to see his reaction to her outfit. To glimpse that smouldering desire in the blue depths of his eyes. To feel her heartbeat increase when he looked at her. To hope for another forbidden kiss.

She drove with care to the function centre and walked through the door at precisely seven-thirty. She casually walked over to the corner of the room and, holding her breath, searched for Jackson. Todd saw her first and waved. He gave her a quick thumbs-up before returning his attention to the person he'd been talking to.

'From the back, you look ravishing,' a deep voice said from directly behind her. His breath fanned down her bare neck and Susie couldn't help the shiver of delight that raced through her. 'I don't know if I'm game enough for you to turn around,' he whispered. 'You have the sexiest legs I've ever seen.'

Susie was thankful the room was now swarming with people as waiters brought out trays of pre-dinner drinks. She had no idea what to say to Jackson. Her mind had gone blank the instant he'd spoken and all she'd been aware of had been the richness of his voice and the emotions he'd stirred in her.

'Are you purposely trying to drive me insane?' he asked as she slowly turned to face him.

'And if I am?' she challenged.

Jackson merely smiled at her. 'Are you flirting with me, Dr Monahan?' he asked, mimicking her question from yesterday. Had it only been yesterday? So much had happened since his arrival in Brisbane. When he was lecturing or away from her, he found himself becoming impatient for time to pass, yet when he was with her he wanted time to slow down so he could savour every second.

Susie laughed, amazed at how a few seconds in his company had increased her excitement. 'Feels a lot like it, from what I can recall.'

'You are…' He paused, his gaze filled with desire as he looked down into her eyes. 'Irresistible.'

'I think I'm moving up in the world,' Susie replied, and at Jackson's frown she continued, 'Well, last night, you said I was captivating. The night before you said I was breath-taking. Tonight, it's irresistible.'

He nodded, a slight smile playing on his lips. 'That's because I remember how good you felt in my arms. I'd give anything right now to take you out of here so we can be— Yes, well, hello again, Mr Petunia.' Jackson quickly changed his tone as he reached over and shook hands with Susie's colleague.

'How did you get on with Hilda Kazinski this afternoon, Susie?' Mr Petunia asked.

Jackson instantly felt like a heel. He'd been so busy ogling Susie that he'd completely forgotten she'd spent the better part of the afternoon performing a difficult piece of surgery. He listened to her reply, glad to hear the patient was doing well.

Moments later they were called in to dinner and Mr Petunia stayed with them as they walked towards their table.

'My wife was going to join me this evening,' he said as he sat down. 'But at the last minute my daughter called up to say two of her children were sick and her husband was on night shift. Well, you come from a large family, Susie, so you know what it's like.'

'Yes, I do.' She smiled.

Their table filled up quickly and conversations began to flow. The MC for the evening stood and welcomed everyone. Shortly afterwards, Jackson made yet another short speech, impressing Susie once more with his diversity. For the past three days, he must have seen the same people several times, at lectures, luncheons and dinners. Still, what he was saying was fresh and enjoyable. She admired him and his professionalism. She also noted that when he sat down again, he moved his chair slightly closer to hers.

Susie tried hard to focus on what Mr Petunia was saying, nodding and smiling politely, all the while unbearably conscious of Jackson. She could feel the pin-pricks of excitement course down her spine, could feel her body crying out for his touch. Her reaction was becoming too intrusive and she sternly told herself to stop it.

'Don't you agree?' Mr Petunia was saying, and Susie hadn't the faintest idea of what he'd been talking about. Once more she'd been so caught up in her awareness of Jackson that her mind seemed unable to function.

She frowned thoughtfully and said, 'Hmm.' And nodded slightly.

'Excuse me,' Jackson said, and Susie quickly turned to give him her attention. He saw an unmistakable hint of passion reflected in her blue eyes and for a moment he lost his train of thought. His gut twisted with delight and despair. Things were starting to get way out of hand. 'Ah...' He frowned and nearly groaned in frustration as her lips parted, her breathing marginally audible as it escaped. He swallowed, watching as her gaze flicked down to his mouth before returning to his eyes.

His sluggish brain registered that she was waiting for him to speak. Although the looks they'd exchanged seemed to have happened in slow motion, Jackson knew it had only been a few seconds. At least, he *hoped* it had. Susie had the ability to make him forget all rational thought and in some ways he resented it. No

other woman had affected him that way before—not even Alison.

He cleared his throat. 'You said there were
several videos in the hospital library of other
hand reconstruction operations you've performed, correct?'

'Yes.' She nodded her head.

'How long ago did you do them?'

She thought for a moment, realising that the
person on the other side of Jackson was also
listening to their conversation. She hoped and
prayed that no one could read the emotions in
her eyes when she looked at the visiting professor! 'One was in February this year and the
other was July. In both cases, though, we've
also videoed the follow-up visits, thereby
keeping a complete record of any of the after-
effects the surgery has had.'

'And you're planning to use this for a new
research project?'

Susie was surprised. How had Jackson
learned about her research plans?

'That's right. I'm currently putting together
a proposal for a new research project and hope
to start on that next year.'

'But haven't the National Health and
Medical Research Foundation grants closed for

this year?' the person on the other side of Jackson asked.

'Yes, they have, but as this research directly follows on from my last grant—'

'They view it more as a continuation,' Jackson finished for her. 'Well done. So I guess you'll be wanting to add Hilda Kazinski to the study.'

'Hopefully. I'll discuss it with her in a few days' time.'

'Good. Actually, as I have tomorrow evening off, I thought I'd watch them. Do you think the hospital library will let me borrow them?'

Susie felt the beginning of a smile twitching at her lips. 'Oh, I'm sure they would.'

Jackson watched her lips, noticing she was trying to suppress a smile. He glanced over his shoulder to see that the person next to him was now talking to someone else. He returned his attention to Susie. 'What?' Even as he asked the question, he could feel the tug of his own lips turning upwards. Her eyes were alive with amusement and his gut twisted again at the sight.

'Oh, nothing,' she replied coyly.

'Come on,' he coaxed, his tone dropping to a more intimate level. He was enjoying teasing her a little.

'I'm just in awe of the glamorous life you lead.'

'Meaning?'

'Meaning that on your only night off in Brisbane, you're choosing to sit in a hotel room and watch a video on hand reconstruction.' She paused, smothering the laugh. 'What a party animal.'

Jackson's smile increased. 'Who said I was going to be sitting in a hotel room?'

'Oh, you mean you're going to watch it somewhere at the hospital? You certainly know how to have a good time.'

'No. Actually...' he leaned in a little closer '...I was planning to watch it at your house.' As he eased back, Jackson took great delight in watching as her amusement slipped away, to be replaced by a startled look as the full impact of his words registered.

He shifted slightly and leaned his arm on the back of his chair. As he did so, his serviette slid to the floor. Bending down to retrieve it, he decided to add fuel to the fire and gently brushed a finger on an exposed part of her calf muscle.

The brief contact made Susie jump, her knee hitting the base of the table, jostling the silver and glassware on top. Conversations stopped. People looked at her. She could feel herself beginning to blush with embarrassment and smiled quickly.

'Sorry. Patellar reflex,' she explained. Everyone returned to what they'd been doing while Susie glanced down at her fingers, which were clenched tightly around her evening bag. She needed to get out of there.

Putting her serviette onto the table, she smiled politely at those around her as she stood. 'Excuse me.' With that, she forced herself not to rush but to walk calmly and steadily away from the table. She could feel Jackson's gaze on her but she forced herself not to care. How could he have put her in such a situation? What had possessed him to touch her in such an intimate manner in company?

Susie's head started to hurt. It had been a long day and as she entered the rest-room for a moment of peace and quiet, she leaned her hands on the bench top and closed her eyes. She was fatigued and on top of that she was desperately fighting her mounting attraction to Jackson.

After a few minutes she felt more in control and better able to cope with the rest of the evening. Taking a deep breath, she headed back, but as she drew closer to the dining room she detoured to the right and through the French doors that led to the balcony.

Breathing in the fresh November air, she gazed out on the lights of Brisbane city. She loved living here. Loved inner city living, as well as being only an hour away from the beautiful hinterland of the Sunshine Coast.

'How's that patellar reflex?'

There was no mistaking Jackson's deep, sensual tone and she didn't bother to glance over her shoulder.

'Better.' She looked the other way.

'Liar,' he accused softly as she felt his arm brush hers. She shivered involuntarily, instantly responding to the light touch.

'I think I'm a better judge of how my patellar reflexes are doing.' Susie was still finding it hard to look at him. She knew the moment she did, her anger would melt away like snow on a hot summer's day.

'That wasn't what I meant and you know it.'

She could tell he had a smile on that gorgeous mouth of his, even without seeing it. She closed her eyes against the image, willing it to go away. It wouldn't. Why was she so in tune with him? Why couldn't she simply switch off her attraction like a light switch?

'Oh?' Susie reluctantly turned to look at him, only to find his face closer than she'd anticipated. 'What was I...?' Her breath trembled a little but she forced herself to continue. Hold onto the anger, she willed herself. Hold onto the anger. 'Expected to say? That the visiting orthopaedic professor was fondling my leg? That would have gone down brilliantly!'

Jackson chuckled and the sound invaded her heart. She looked away from him but he gently reached over, cupped her chin and urged her face back around. 'Let's get one thing straight.' The taste of his breath held a hint of the red wine they'd been served, and Susie savoured it. 'I didn't *fondle* your leg.'

For one blinding second, Susie thought he was denying having touched her in the first place. Had he touched her? Had she just imagined it?

'I *caressed* it,' he confessed with a laugh that turned into a groan as he recalled just how perfect she'd felt beneath his touch. 'There's a big difference.'

Susie sighed, clinging vainly to her rapidly dissolving anger. 'Well, you still shouldn't have done it.'

'I couldn't help myself.' He shrugged, frowning as he did so.

'Next time try harder!'

'Look, Susie, I'm sorry.'

He touched his hand to her shoulder but removed it the instant she glared at him. They were in public view. Anyone might see them talking intimately together. She edged to the side a little, hoping to put more distance between them.

'I didn't know you were going to react like that. Honestly.'

His tone was so sincere, she knew she'd already forgiven him. 'It's all right.' She turned to look out over the city. They were both silent for a few minutes, a comfortable, companionable silence while they soaked up the beautiful, warm night.

'It's nice here,' he stated. 'In Brisbane, I mean.'

'Yeah.'

'How long have you lived here?' Despite the attraction between them, Jackson had to keep reminding himself that he really didn't know Susie all that well.

'In Brisbane? About five years now.'

'Do you like it here? I mean, do you have any plans to leave?'

Susie glanced at him, curiously. 'I love it here.' Her answer was a little hesitant as she wasn't quite sure why he was asking. Was he thinking of asking her to come to Melbourne to visit him? Whoa! She forced her thoughts back into a neat and orderly line. 'I'm close to my family and good friends. The weather here is gorgeous for seven months out of twelve and even the winter isn't so bad. I think the only things I don't like are the fruit bats and the blue-tongue and bearded lizards.' She shuddered and Jackson laughed. 'But they're more common at my parents' property.'

'It sounds nice. Lizards, bats and all.'

She laughed, enjoying just being with him.

'You mentioned that you'd worked in Asia. When was that?'

'What's with the twenty questions?'

'I just want to get to know you a little better.'

'Jackson, you leave here on Saturday evening. That's three days away.'

'I know. Which is why I want to make the most of the time we have together.' He glanced at her and then back out to the electrically lit

view. 'You've become…special to me and
I—'

'Susan?'

Susie whirled around, her shock catching in
her throat as she looked into Walter's green
eyes.

'I've been waiting for you to come back inside.' Walter crossed to her side and placed a
possessive arm around her waist. 'Surprise,
darling.' He leaned down and kissed her
cheek, catching her off guard. Then he held a
hand out to Jackson. 'Hello. I'm Walter
Amery, Susan's fiancé.'

The blood pounded fiercely in Susie's head
as she looked at Jackson, then Walter and back
to Jackson again. This wasn't happening. This
simply wasn't happening.

CHAPTER EIGHT

'SUSAN'S fiancé?' Jackson asked ever so politely. He glanced down at Susie, noting how uncomfortable she was with this jerk's arm about her. His first instinct had been to slog Walter Amery right between the eyes, but his mother had always taught him that violence wasn't the civilised way to express one's feelings.

His second instinct was to pluck Susie from the other man's reach and cradle her protectively within his own arms. That was probably the better option to go with but he was sure she wouldn't like it, especially as it would bring unwanted attention to the true feelings between them.

His third option was to remain calm and unaffected whilst managing to get Susie as far away from Walter as possible…and he knew *just* how to do it. Taking in the pristine penguin suit the other man was wearing, noting the perfection of his hair and the shine on his shoes, Jackson had already sized Walter

192

Amery up as a man who liked to be thought prestigious.

Jackson smiled warmly and placed his hand in Walter's, ensuring his grip was firm and positive. 'Pleased to meet you, Walter. I'm Jackson Myers.'

'My goodness,' Walter said as he peered closer. 'So you are. I apologise, Professor. I didn't recognise you.'

Susie's gaze narrowed. She'd watched Jackson carefully during those first few moments and had seen his 'official mask' slip into place.

Jackson took a step around Susie so that he was now facing Walter. 'Are you an orthopaedic surgeon as well?'

'Good gracious, no,' Walter said, as though being labelled an orthopod was a disease. Susie rolled her eyes and sighed, stepping slightly out of Walter's embrace. Thankfully, he dropped his arm and tugged on his jacket lapels. 'I'm a plastic surgeon.'

'I see.' Jackson nodded. 'You must be here from interstate, then.'

'No. no. I'm consulting privately now at the Goldtown Private Hospital.'

Here he goes again, Susie thought as Walter preened openly. She wondered why she hadn't seen his selfishness from the beginning. It was in the past and she was definitely over him now. When he'd touched her, all she'd felt had been a shuddering revulsion.

'Oh, but of course you're not from Brisbane,' Walter continued when Jackson failed to be impressed by the hospital name. 'It is *the* most prestigious private hospital in Queensland. We have people from all over the state and some from interstate coming to our hospital specifically for the first-class treatment they receive.'

Jackson frowned and glanced from Susie to Walter and back to Susie again. Had she lied to him? She'd said that her fiancé, or more correctly her *ex*-fiancé, had left the state. What type of game was she playing? As Walter continued to drone on about his work, Jackson wondered what she'd seen in him. He was boring. Then again, perhaps Susie liked boring and monotonous men but, he reminded himself, not for the first time, he really didn't know her that well.

He now had a lot of unanswered questions…questions he was determined to have answered before he left. What game was she playing? She was attracted to *him*. No one could share a kiss as they had that afternoon and be unaffected by it. He'd asked her directly whether she was seeing someone and she'd said no. That could only mean that Mr Excitement here was lying. Perhaps Walter wanted Susie back? Would she go? After all, he himself would be gone at the end of the week and she'd be alone again.

The thought of leaving Susie in the clutches of a man like Walter Amery chilled him to the bone. A wild longing to kidnap Susie and take her back to Melbourne with him passed fleetingly through his mind.

He looked at her again, only to see her unsuccessfully try to smother a yawn. Then he remembered the hectic day she'd already had and his annoyance turned to compassion. She should be tucked up in bed, sleeping. He'd have to get Walter away from her, then she could escape. They would talk later.

'Tell me, Walter,' Jackson said as he stepped around to the man's other side, thereby leaving Susie as free as a bird, 'were you involved in setting up this prestigious hospital? I mean, if I wanted to do something like this back in Melbourne, how would I go about it?'

Susie couldn't believe Jackson was serious. Was that what he wanted to do when he got back to Melbourne? Set up a high-class hospital for high-class people, their only aim being to make loads of money? She felt cheated that he could be so shallow. Then again, she hadn't seen the trait in Walter until it had been too late.

Walter turned his back to her so he was now facing Jackson, talking animatedly about his precious hospital. Susie was the type of doctor who'd entered the profession because of her great need to help people, not exploit them for money. She shook her head in disgust, unwilling to listen to Walter any longer. She was leaving. She'd had enough.

Not wanting to interrupt their *tête-à-tête*, she shrugged and slipped quietly away. For an instant she thought she'd felt Jackson's gaze follow her movements, but when she glanced over her shoulder he was listening intently to Walter.

Not bothering to say goodbye to anyone, she returned to her car and wearily drove home. It was too late for her bubble bath. Once inside, she merely stripped off her glamorous clothes, brushed her teeth and pulled on a pair of boxer shorts and a singlet top before climbing between the sheets.

*   *   *

Susie managed to concentrate during most of Thursday but as the day wore on she started to become more and more nervous. Had Jackson meant what he'd said? Was he still planning to come around to her place that evening to watch the videos of her hand and microsurgery reconstructions?

She'd managed ward round and clinic without a problem, as well as getting a debrief from Kyle on the status of Blade Fargo. So far there had been no complications with his surgery and it looked as though he was going to make an uncomplicated recovery.

'Apparently,' Kyle told her, 'he's quite impressed with our Patti. He's asked her to stay on as his private nurse for the rest of the movie shoot.'

'Good.' Susie nodded sternly. 'That way we can be sure his arm won't be exacerbated. Patti knows what to keep an eye out for.'

'Good heavens, Susie. Don't you see the underlying meaning here?'

'What?' Susie frowned at her registrar, focusing on his face as his words started to sink in. 'What's the underlying meaning?'

'That Blade Fargo and Patti are a couple.'

'Really!' Susie was surprised. 'So soon? They've only known each other a few days.'

'I think this could be serious,' Kyle told her. 'Besides, it doesn't take more than a few days to fall in love when you meet the right person.'

'Oh? And so how many times have *you* been in love, then, Dr Thompson?'

'Ah...not that I'm speaking from my own experience,' he clarified quickly. 'It's just that seeing them together is so nice. They really care about each other.' Kyle shook his own head as he mused out loud. 'You know, I thought Blade would be a stuck-up snob but he's not. He's so down to earth. He's an actor and his job is to act. That's it.'

'Wouldn't Patti get jealous of his leading ladies?'

'Surprisingly not. The actress he's in the movie with came by this morning so they could rehearse and Patti didn't seem at all bothered when the script called for a kiss.'

Susie raised her eyebrows. 'Well good for her, then.'

'That's just what I think.' Kyle stood up. 'Are you taking Hilda Kazinski back to Theatre today?'

'It all depends,' Susie replied. 'At the moment, I don't think so. The surgery I performed yesterday needs a bit more time to heal. I'll see how she's looking later on in the day.

Chances are, she's a fast healer.' It would also give her the excuse to cancel her plans with Jackson.

'Do you want me to organise further scanning for this afternoon so we can check it out?'

'Sure. Thanks, Kyle.' When her registrar didn't move she looked at him expectantly. 'Was there anything else?'

'No. Not really.' He stood and took a few steps towards the door before pausing. 'It's just you.' He frowned at her. 'I'm concerned about you. You're not your usual self today.'

Susie forced a smile. 'I'm fine. I guess it's just the added strain of having the VOP here this week, that's all. Everything will be back to normal next week.'

'Good.' Kyle seemed satisfied with her answer and took himself off. Susie worked on her research proposal right through lunchtime and into the afternoon. She refused to allow her mind to dwell on Jackson or the fact that he might walk through her door at any moment.

A few minutes later, there was a brief knock on her door before it opened, the sounds making her jump violently. Her heart thudded wildly against her ribs and her mouth went dry with anticipation. Was this Jackson?

Todd walked in and she sighed with a mixture of relief and disappointment. Todd watched her carefully for a moment before closing the door. 'Expecting someone else?' he teased.

'No,' she answered quickly, then, unable to fight the strain any longer, she tossed her pen down and raised her hand to massage her temples. 'He told me last night that he was coming to watch videos at my house tonight.'

'Really?' Todd's eyebrows hit his hairline. 'Going to book a romantic comedy?'

Susie gave a short hysterical laugh. 'No. Professor Myers wants to watch the videos on hand surgery.'

'The ones in the library?'

'Yes.'

'Wow! He sure knows how to show a girl a good time. Why are you on edge, then?'

'Because Jackson is going to be in my home!' she exclaimed, flinging her hands around wildly.

'Whoa. Settle down there. Control your agitation. What's so wrong with Jackson coming around to your house? From where I'm sitting, it's about time you two got to spend some time alone. Think about it, Susie. In the past few days, you've either been at lectures, luncheons, dinners or operating. What time have you had for serious discussions and get-to-know-you conversations? I'll tell you,' he continued when she opened her mouth to reply. 'Absolutely none.'

'But there's no point. He'll be gone on Saturday evening and then what?'

'I don't know, Susie.' Todd's voice was quiet and sincere. 'You tell me. How do you feel about him?'

'I... I...' She sighed and tucked a stray curl behind her ear. 'I don't know,' she admitted eventually. 'It's all happened so quickly that I'm not sure *what* I think.'

'I didn't ask how you *think*, my dear boss, I asked how you *feel*.'

She smiled at him and shook her head. 'To tell you the truth, Todd, it's something I've been trying hard not to focus on.'

'Why? Because you don't think Jackson feels the same way? Has the same intense emotions you're obviously experiencing?'

'Who are you? What have you done with my secretary?' Susie laughed before she narrowed her gaze at him. 'Do you have a part-time job writing a column for a magazine giving out advice to the lovelorn?'

Todd smiled. 'No, I don't, and stop changing the subject. Richard told me yesterday that Jackson has bitten his head off more times in Brisbane than anywhere else in the world, and when Richard tried to schedule something for tonight, Jackson firmly insisted that he be permitted his scheduled night off to do whatever he chose. He hasn't even told Richard where he's going and has said he would leave his pager and mobile phone at the hotel.'

'Oh, no,' Susie groaned and covered her face with her hands. 'That means he's coming over.'

'I'd say that it does.'

'So Richard doesn't know what's going on?'

'No.'

'And you're not going to tell him, are you,' she stated firmly.

'What am *I* supposed to tell him? *You* don't even know what's going on.' Todd laughed when she groaned again. 'Listen, Susie, you've just got to relax and go with the flow. Live a little. Take a chance and don't punish him for past mistakes. Remember that Jackson isn't like Walter or Greg.'

'Ha. That's what you think. Jackson was talking quite animatedly with Walter last night about how to set up a private hospital.'

'Walter was at the dinner last night?'

'Yes.'

'Why?'

'Who knows?' Her tone was bored and impersonal. 'I certainly don't and I didn't stick around to find out.'

'Perhaps Jackson was just being polite.'

Susie had thought about that as well. She couldn't bring herself to believe that Jackson was the type of doctor who was in the profession solely for the money. Sure, the VOP would have brought him international acclaim and prestige but he'd been so eager to help out with Blade Fargo's surgery that she had taken that as proof that he was a doctor first and foremost because he wanted to help people. Just like her. He'd explained that the VOP had been his wife's idea and he'd only gone through with it to carry out her wishes. His tribute to the departed love of his life.

'I don't know any more.' She sighed again and picked up her pen.

'So what are you going to do?'

Susie shrugged. 'I'm going to wait. Wait and see if he calls or simply turns up.'

Todd picked up the files in her out-tray and chuckled as he walked to the door. 'Ah, ain't love grand?'

'Love!' She choked. 'Who said anything about love?'

Todd merely laughed and walked out.

'Love?' she whispered, and then quickly shook her head. 'No! Not love. Not again. Not this little black duck,' she said with determination.

She was still telling herself that as she unlocked her front door a few hours later. She'd heard nothing from Jackson so obviously he'd decided not to keep their…their what? Date? She'd hardly call it that.

She hurried to her room and kicked off her shoes, pulling the clip out of her hair at the same time. Now that he wasn't coming around, perhaps she could have that bubble bath she'd missed out on last night. It felt *so* good not to have to go out this evening. She glanced at the clock—seven-thirty.

She changed out of her suit into a loose, flowing skirt and top, taking time to brush her hair before heading to the kitchen for a drink. She eyed the choice of soothing herbal teas in her cupboard while she waited for the kettle to boil and eventually chose chamomile. She checked the kitchen clock—seven-thirty-five.

'Oh, stop it,' she told herself as she ran a hand through her hair, but it was easier said than done. She was anxious and on edge. Would he come or wouldn't he? Perhaps she should call him?

When the doorbell rang she jumped in fright. She stood, glued to the spot for a whole minute, wondering what she should do. Was it him? Was it someone else? With her heart pounding rapidly, she smoothed her hands down her skirt, telling herself there was nothing to be concerned about, and forced her legs to carry her towards the door.

The doorbell rang again as she reached for the handle, giving her a fright, and she gave a little scream. She opened the door to see Jackson standing on the other side of the screen door. She knew that the screen mesh shielded her from Jackson's view but she could certainly see him and he looked...sexy.

He was wearing a navy polo shirt and the same denim jeans she'd seen him in the other night—the ones that fitted him to perfection.

'Susie? What's the matter? Open the door. Why did you scream?' His impatient tone made her fumble with the key for the screen door but finally she managed. He didn't wait for her to open it but wrenched the handle down the instant he heard the lock click.

He stormed in, almost knocking her over, glancing around the hallway. 'What's the matter?' he asked again.

'Nothing.' She concentrated on locking the screen door before closing the wooden door. Unable to delay the inevitable any more, she turned to face him. The look in his eyes was unmistakably raw with repressed desire and involuntarily she parted her lips, her breathing instantly erratic.

His gaze travelled the length of her and her insides spiralled with warmth. Nothing could have made her look away from him at that heart-stopping moment, and before she could utter a word Jackson dropped his bag and hauled her into his arms, his mouth moving hungrily over hers.

In contrast to the kiss they'd shared the previous day, this one was hot and hungry, leaving Susie in little doubt as to just how attracted to her Jackson was. His hands roved over her back as he deepened the kiss. She went with him, eager to keep up, eager to show him just how mutual the desire was.

He groaned and urged her backwards and soon she felt the coolness of the wall against her back. He leaned in, his body pressing against her own, and she felt her breasts crushed against the firmness of his chest.

The smell of raw, unleashed craving mingled between them as the need for more rose urgently in both of them. She dug her fingers into his shoulder blades before sliding them firmly down his back, feeling the flexed muscles beneath. Wanting to touch him, she impatiently tugged his shirt from the waistband of his jeans, her fingers now itching to make contact with his skin.

When the task was finally completed, she moaned with delight when she reached her objective. His skin was hot to her touch just as she'd known it would be. Giving in to the yearning that had been building within her since early Monday morning, she allowed her hands to explore the solid contours of his torso, committing each one to memory.

Jackson groaned against her mouth, unable to believe how this woman could set him on fire. The sensations he was experiencing were all completely foreign but he was definitely enjoying each new one she discovered. The touch of her hands on his body, the way her mouth was responding to his, giving in to every one of his needs, matching them eagerly.

She lifted one leg slightly and coiled it around the back of his before sliding it slowly down to the ground. The action caused a stirring deep within him and he could feel himself losing control of the situation. She repeated the action and he groaned with longing.

Breaking his mouth free, they both gasped in air before he pushed her hair aside and smothered the smoothness of her neck in hot, feverish kisses. He then changed direction and dipped towards the exposed skin above her breasts.

Her hands slid out from his shirt and at the same time she murmured his name. 'Mmm,' she sighed, lacing her fingers through his hair. 'Jackson.'

The way she said his name pierced right to his heart and he realised that things were getting out of control. He worked his way up, not wanting to break the contact immediately but knowing he must—and soon. He nipped at her ear lobe and she giggled. The sound was intensely provocative and the last thing he needed at that moment.

'Susie.' With his breathing still out of control, he looked down at her face. Her eyes were closed, her parted lips were dark pink and swollen from his kisses, her breathing as ragged as his own. She was a vision of loveliness. Unable to resist, he brushed his lips against hers, forcing himself not to deepen the kiss.

'Mmm,' she murmured again, and when he brushed them a third time, her hands clamped themselves on either side of his head and held his lips where they belonged. Seductively, she ran her tongue over his lips and was thrilled with the shudder that tore through his body.

Ever so slowly, she kissed him again. Teasing and testing, refusing to deepen the kiss.

'Susie.' This time her name was torn from his lips and she was satisfied with the response. 'Honey…'

She kissed him again, not wanting him to speak for she'd already sensed his slow but sure withdrawal. Even though their bodies were still pressed firmly together, Jackson had already mentally distanced himself. She didn't want to think about things rationally and if they stopped completely, they'd have to talk things through.

Susie just wanted to go on feeling exactly as she was feeling now, not caring about her already bruised heart or the fact that the man in her arms would be leaving within forty-eight hours.

She breathed slowly against his mouth before tasting him once again. Now that she knew how incredible they were together, it was something she knew she'd crave for the rest of her life.

He didn't break free and he didn't hurry her. Instead, he took what she was offering but held himself under rigid control, still marvelling at how easily he'd lost his perspective. Perhaps the building resistance they'd been employing for the past four days had increased his drive. Whatever this was between them, Jackson knew he'd never experience anything like it again. This was unique.

Knowing the moment had come where she couldn't hang onto the physical pull any longer, Susie lowered her hands to his shoulders and slowly opened her eyes. His blue eyes were gazing down into hers, the fire still burning but gradually being doused.

Neither of them spoke but the communication was there. As their breathing steadied to a more normal pace, Jackson reluctantly eased himself away from her. For one fleeting instant, he thought Susie might overrule him and drag his body back where it belonged. Instead, she let her hands fall limply to her sides, her gaze dipping briefly to his lips before she looked down at the floor.

He felt awful. How could he have done what he just had? She was a colleague and, despite how much he was attracted to her, he owed her the respect and common decency he'd show other female colleagues. Guilt started to swamp him and he opened his mouth, an apology on his lips.

'Don't.' Susie held up her hand. 'Don't apologise. We both wanted it, we both needed it and we'll both take responsibility for it.'

'You're right, but I was also going to say I'd never meant it to happen.'

'Liar.' She crossed her arms defensively over her body, rubbing her bare arms, her body still feeling bereft of his touch. She turned and headed into the living room, leaving him to follow her or stay where he was. She needed to sit down.

'Why am I a liar?' He could feel the faint strain of annoyance surge through him at her accusation. He picked up his bag and followed her. She was sitting with her legs tucked beneath her skirt on a large floral chair. Her hands were clenched tightly in her lap and her eyes were momentarily closed.

Susie fought for composure before opening her eyes to look at him. 'Because you *did* mean that kiss to happen. You may not have *realised* it, but it's been building ever since we met on Monday morning.' She shrugged, displaying a nonchalance she didn't feel. 'It was…inevitable.'

He registered the truth of her words as he slumped down into the matching floral chair. 'When you opened the door to let me in, I guess everything became too much to control. I was relieved we could see each other without being surrounded by people. I was still trying to resist you because I knew it wasn't the right thing to do and I was slightly annoyed because of that boring jerk you used to be engaged to.'

'What's Walter got to do with this?'

'How could you have been engaged to someone like that?' The question had been buzzing around in his brain ever since he'd met the self-centred bore the night before.

'Don't you criticise me,' she replied hotly, feeling her temper begin to rise. She wasn't that surprised. With all the turbulent emotions still bubbling deep inside, it was little wonder she was reacting so erratically.

'I wasn't.' Jackson eyed her warily and realised she was like a dormant volcano just waiting to explode. Amazingly, he couldn't think of a time when she'd looked more beautiful. Her eyes were hot with fire, her cheeks were flushed with colour and her shoulders were ramrod straight, showing she was spoiling for a fight. 'I was surprised to find you'd been engaged to him and I was wondering why you'd lied to me.'

'What! When did I lie to you? How dare you call me a liar?'

'Why not? You just called me one.' He stood and started to pace around the room.

'That was different and you know it.' She watched him carefully.

'You told me your fiancé had moved to Sydney after you'd broken up.'

'He did.'

'They why did Walter tell me he's been in Brisbane for the past few years?'

'Because he has.'

'What?' Jackson's voice cracked with exasperation.

'I was engaged twice!' Susie flung her arms out wide. Her words obviously had a sobering effect on Jackson because he stopped pacing and stared at her in amazement.

'You've been engaged twice?'

'Yes. First to Walter and then to Greg.'

He exhaled sharply, shoving one hand in his pocket and running the other hand through his hair. 'No wonder.' His words were barely audible but Susie caught them.

'No wonder what?' she asked instantly, her chin jutting up in defiance.

'No wonder you're so afraid of getting hurt again.' His tone was filled with such compassion that her anger melted away. 'Did you break off either engagement?'

'No.'

'Why did Walter break up with you?'

Susie crossed her arms in front of her chest. 'Are the twenty questions really necessary?'

'I think so.'

'Am I allowed the same courtesy?'

His gaze narrowed marginally but, he realised, it was only fair. 'Of course.' He was starting to itch again—itching to touch her. Just to hold her hand in his, to feel her smooth skin against his own, to be close enough to drink in her perfume. She was like a drug and, he was beginning to realise, he was slowly becoming addicted.

CHAPTER NINE

SUSIE made them both a cup of tea, while Jackson watched her flit around her kitchen like a nervous butterfly.

'How's Hilda Kazinski doing?' he asked, trying to fill the strained atmosphere with a bit of conversation. She gave him an update before she thought of a question of her own.

'How did you know where I lived? I never gave you my address.'

'Todd,' he replied as she handed him the mug. He took a sip, staying where he was for a moment. 'He knows there's something going on between us, doesn't he,' he stated. Susie looked up from stirring her tea.

'What makes you ask?'

'He didn't ask why I needed your address and promised he wouldn't say a word to Richard.'

'He guessed.' Susie shrugged as she walked through to the lounge room. This time she sat at one end of the lounge and Jackson sat at the other, facing each other. 'So you want to talk about my past?'

At his nod, she continued. 'We'll start with Walter, shall we? He wasn't as pretentious back then as he is now,' Susie explained, trying to keep her emotions under control. Every time she thought about her failed engagements, it only increased her feelings of inadequacy.

Now she was dredging them all back up again and why? Because Jackson wanted to know. For some reason it was important and the more she talked, the more she found she *wanted* to tell him.

'We worked on a research project together and then after about six months we realised everyone thought of us as a couple. Not long after that he proposed and as it was the first proposal I'd received, I accepted.' She looked away for a moment, wondering how she could have made such a drastic mistake.

'Did he love you?' Jackson's tone was gentle.

'He never said it but he was always very thoughtful and, well…coming from a family of ten children, I knew I wanted children and…'

'Your biological clock was ticking?' he guessed, and she nodded.

'So when did Walter break it off?'

'When he realised I wouldn't forgo my career for his. He told me he needed a wife who not only understood his work but who looked good on his arm. I was merely decoration.' She turned away, unable to control the stab of pain she felt.

'He really hurt you, didn't he?' Jackson reached out to take her hand in his.

'It's not *him* who's causing the pain now but my disbelief in my own stupidity. Eight months later, I met Greg. He was a general surgeon and was completely opposite to Walter. He was wild and funny and we had lots of laughs together. After four short weeks, he proposed. He told me I was beautiful but that he also admired me for my intellect. I guess because he was giving me everything Walter hadn't, I thought I'd struck gold. Silly me—I believed him. Then again, so did every other girl in the hospital.'

'Ouch.' Jackson winced. 'He two-timed you?'

'Two-timed, three-timed, probably about six-timed for all I know. When I eventually found out and confronted him, he was blasé about it, as though it wasn't an uncommon thing. When I told him I wouldn't stand for any more infidelities, he accused me of being frigid and informed me he was moving to Sydney. His six-month contract at the hospital had expired and he was out of there.'

'And that was six months ago.' Jackson turned her hand over in his, smoothing his fingers along the softness of her skin. How dared they make Susie think she was to blame for their own inadequacies?

'Yes.' Susie closed her eyes, focusing on the way repeated floods of tingles were travelling up her arm and bursting throughout her body at his caressing touch.

'Do you know why Walter was there last night?'

She opened her eyes slowly, frowning as she did so. 'No. Admittedly, I haven't given it much thought.' Her mind had been otherwise engaged, trying desperately to fight off the attraction she felt towards Jackson!

'Well, I do.'

'What?'

'Yes. He told me that he'd made a grave mistake and was planning to win you back.'

A smile twitched at the corners of Susie's mouth and a bubble of disbelieving laughter rose quickly. She tried to choke it down but was unsuccessful. 'You're joking.'

'No.' He shook his head for added emphasis but inside Jackson swallowed his relief. At least she wasn't going to be taken in again by that dimwit. Couldn't Walter see there was more to Susie than beauty? That she deserved a challenging career? And from what he'd seen, she was extremely good at what she did. Microsurgery was a difficult sub-speciality and he'd been highly impressed with the papers he'd read of Susie's during the past few days. Richard had been a little puzzled when he'd asked him to find them but Jackson hadn't been in the mood to answer his aide's questions.

'Well, I'd better formulate a plan to change his mind, don't you think?' She laughed again, still unable to believe Walter was that stupid. Why would he think she'd want him back? Probably because she was still single and she could bet Walter thought he'd come charging in on his white horse and rescue her.

'It's nice to see you smiling again.' Unable to stop himself, Jackson reached out and caressed her cheek. She was amazing. 'I admire you.'

The laughter slowly dissolved from Susie's eyes and they continued to look at each other. 'Why?' she eventually asked.

'Why do I admire you?' At her nod, he continued, 'Because after two bad experiences, you've managed to pick yourself up and keep on going with your life.'

'Yeah, but my experiences are nothing compared to what you've been through.' Her words were filled with sympathy. He must have gone through the most terrible ordeal yet here he was, daring to live again.

Jackson dropped his hand and shook his head. 'I felt like dying. When I heard the news, I...' He paused and swallowed. Now it was Susie's turn to hold his hand. 'I wanted to die as well.'

'I'm very glad you didn't. Think of all the people you've met during the past year on the visiting professorship. Think of how many lives you've touched, how many people you've helped. Last night, Jackson...' Susie wasn't sure whether this was the right time to confess it or not but she was going to. 'When I left, you were talking with Walter so animatedly about his ridiculous private hospital that I thought you might be the same as him.'

'I'm not,' he denied instantly.

'I realised that.'

'I was only getting him to talk so you could get away. You looked terrible.'

'Thanks a lot.'

He smiled. 'You know what I mean. I knew
you'd had an extremely busy day and the last
thing you needed was Mr Non-Excitement annoying you.'

'Thanks,' she replied, her tone a little
clipped. She could handle Walter by herself.

'What now?' Jackson asked, not at all
fooled by her attitude.

She hesitated, unsure what to say. He
seemed to know her so well, reading her body
language and seeing the truth of her feelings
in her eyes. It was disconcerting to be around
a person who seemed to know her so well,
especially in such a short time.

'Why were you so concerned with wanting
to get me away from Walter? Was it just because he introduced himself as my fiancé?'

'That and, as I said, you looked tired.'

'I don't need you to protect me, Jackson, or
fight my battles for me.'

'I didn't. Personally, I thought I behaved
with the utmost restraint. My first instinct was
to slam my fist right into Walter's face.'

Susie's eyes opened wide in shock.

'But I didn't. I could see that you were tired
and didn't need the added complication so I
distracted him. That's all.'

'Chivalry? I thought that was dead,' she mused. 'Do you always protect females or just the ones you think can't fend for themselves?'

Her words were tainted with irony and he opened his mouth to answer but then closed it, thinking for a moment. He'd always been protective of his little sisters and knew they had resented it at times, but he was their brother. It was part of his responsibility to look out for them. So, too, his mother, especially since his father's death.

'You might be right,' he confessed, taking Susie completely off guard. 'I've always protected my sisters and my mother. Alison welcomed it as well, leaving me to solve any problems that came our way.'

Susie noted the way his voice softened when he mentioned his wife, the way his eyes flicked down momentarily to their hands which were still entwined. A fraction of a second later, he let go and Susie recoiled from the action as though he'd slapped her. Alison—the ghost in his life. Alison—the woman he'd married.

She bit her tongue to stop herself from asking the question that was burning in her heart. She didn't want to cause him any extra stress but then she remembered that he'd started this twenty-questions game and had agreed she was entitled to some questions of her own.

She took a deep breath and said softly, 'What was she like?'

He waited so long to answer that for a moment she didn't think he was going to. She regretted asking him. The last thing she wanted to do was to cause him extra pain, but it was too late to retract it.

'She had short blonde hair and brown eyes.' His words were stilted as though it pained him to remember. 'She always brought out the best in people, finding their weaknesses and somehow turning them into strengths. She knew this visiting professorship would be good for me and she was right. Little did she know the constant pressure of it would help me get over her death.'

Jackson finally met Susie's gaze. 'I've never spoken to anyone about her like this—not even my sisters. Before I left it was all raw but now…' He reached for her hand again and she couldn't have stopped him even if she'd wanted to. 'Susie, the last woman I kissed before you was Alison.' He paused for a moment, a small smile twitching at his lips. 'Well, actually, it was my mother—but I mean a passionate kiss.'

Susie laughed, the tension easing out of her body. 'I know what you meant.'

'This isn't easy for me,' he confessed, his face serious once more. 'Just as I know it's not easy for you.' He squeezed her hand. 'I'll be gone in forty-eight hours. Back on the tour and then back to my life in Melbourne. Returning home is something I've craved for months now. Initially, I couldn't wait to get away, now I can't wait to get back.'

'So you've said.'

'Susie…I want to spend together whatever free time we have left. It's only going to be an hour here or half an hour there, I know, but what do you say? I'm really looking forward to our drive on Saturday to meet your friends.' He tried hard to interpret the expression on her face but she dipped her head, her hair falling across her cheek.

'We both have a hectic schedule tomorrow.' She was trying hard to carefully choose her words. She didn't want him to think she didn't want to spend time with him because she did, but she also needed to gauge how much time would be enough for her to hold onto her sanity. Self-preservation was a key factor in her life, especially with her track record with relationships. 'I'll more than likely be doing

Hilda Kazinski's next operation while you're doing your last theatre stint of ''show and tell''.'

He chuckled at her wording. 'That's exactly how it feels sometimes.'

'What if I pick you up around sevenish on Saturday morning? I know a nice place on the outskirts of Brisbane that serves a great breakfast.'

Jackson nodded. 'That sounds great.'

Her phone rang. She didn't want to move. She wanted to stay right where she was, with Jackson holding her hand, smiling at her and gazing into her eyes. After a heartbeat they both moved at the same time, and Susie stood to silence the intrusion. She walked into the hall towards the phone. 'It's probably Kyle with his latest report on Blade Fargo,' she murmured as she reached for the receiver. 'Dr Monahan.'

Her eyes widened with surprise and she covered the mouthpiece. 'It's Walter,' she whispered, and Jackson rolled his eyes.

'Tell him you're busy and you have no interest in him whatsoever,' he suggested rather loudly.

'Uh…sorry, Walter. I didn't catch that.'

Walter sighed in exasperation. 'Please, focus, Susan. I need to see you. How is Saturday morning? I can fit you in around ten-fifteen.'

'Sorry. I'm busy Saturday. Listen, why don't I call you next week and we can arrange a time then?' she suggested. He listed a few more times when he was free but she rejected them all, reiterating she'd call him later. She didn't want to break the bad news to him over the phone, deciding it would be better done in person, but with his persistence she was sorely tempted to change her mind.

'Why didn't you simply tell him you're entertaining another man?' Jackson teased when she returned. He'd made himself comfortable, kicking off his shoes and slouching back in the soft cushions. 'He would have got the hint.' He held out his hand and she went to him, sitting down beside him, feeling comfortable and cosy when he settled his arm around her shoulders, the television remote control in his free hand.

'Ready to watch your brilliant skill as a surgeon?' he asked, pressing a button on the remote.

'I thought you were joking. We're not really going to sit here and watch this. It goes on for two and a half hours.'

Jackson laughed and snuggled closer. 'Sounds fine to me so long as we can order some Chinese or something. I'm starting to get hungry!'

Susie marvelled at how relaxed and at home he seemed. He was probably so sick and tired of living out of a hotel that a real home was almost something of a novelty.

Moments later the operating theatre came into focus and there she was, standing at the operating table, explaining the finer points of what she was about to do. She felt self-conscious watching herself, never having sat through a viewing of the tapes before, but with Jackson asking her questions she found herself reaching for the remote to pause it while they discussed things in more detail.

It was liberating to be able to sit down with a man and discuss a subject she was passionate about. He seemed to be really interested and the knowledge thrilled her. Finally she'd met a man who respected her as an intellectual equal, and with that knowledge Susie felt immensely happy.

Her neck hurt. As the pain sent signals to her brain Susie shifted slightly, but the pain continued. It felt as though someone was pinching her neck and she wished they'd stop. It was a mosquito, she realised, and swatted it away. No. The pain was still there.

Slowly she was drawn out of the dream state to reality. The pain in her neck still there and annoying. She must be sleeping at an odd angle. She shifted slightly, only to come up against a hard obstacle.

Had she left her books on the bed again? She kicked at them with her leg but they didn't fall. She kicked them harder, only to hear them groan. Groan! Books didn't groan! Susie frowned. She felt with her foot and realised with a start that it wasn't a book but a leg!

Her eyes snapped open and she tried desperately to focus. She was in her lounge room, the television still on, hissing quietly with black and white snow. She was lying against the back of the lounge suite, her legs entwined with Jackson's, his arm holding her possessively to his body. Jackson! Oh, no. They'd been watching her reconstruction video together.

She scrambled into an upright position, shaking him fiercely. 'Wake up.' She shook him. 'Jackson. Wake up.' With the tiny beams of light peeking from behind her thick curtains, she guessed it to be quite early in the morning.

'Huh?' He slowly moved, stretching languorously. His body was lean and hard as his muscles tensed firmly before he relaxed. His leg brushed hers, igniting a spark she'd been trying to repress ever since he'd arrived last night. He shifted to a sitting position beside her and peered blearily into her eyes.

'Mmm.' With his eyes half closed, he leant over and kissed her soundly on the mouth. 'Hi, there.' His voice was deep and low. 'Guess we must have dozed off.' He reached for her, gathering her into his arms. She resisted him, but only slightly. He nuzzled her neck. 'You're a cuddly girl at heart, aren't you?'

Susie smiled. The embarrassment from their impromptu night on the lounge faded a little. How could she resist when he said such nice things? 'What makes you say that?'

'The way you cuddled into me last night.' He gave her a little squeeze before glancing at the television. 'How long did you say that video went on for?'

Susie chuckled. 'About two and half hours. Must have been pretty boring.'

Jackson laughed, a deep rumbling sound that she felt vibrate through him. 'Not necessarily. Perhaps we were both exhausted.'

'It has been an incredibly hectic week,' she replied as she went to move from his arms.

'Where are you going?'

'To turn the TV off. I can't stand it any more.'

'Why not? You've slept all night with it on.'

'You know what I mean.'

'No, wait,' he said, shifting to the right and sticking his leg out to the side. He was concentrating and she realised he was trying to reach the remote control with his foot. He reached down with his free arm and Susie laughed.

'Let me get it.'

'No. I've almost got it.' He reached over further before crowing triumphantly as he snatched it up into his hand. 'Done.' He pointed it at the set and soon the room was plunged into silence.

It was then Susie noticed the readout on the video clock. 'What? That can't be right.' She grabbed Jackson's wrist and turned it around to read the time on his watch. 'Ten to eight! I'm due at work in ten minutes' time!'

Susie sprang from his arms and rushed out of the room. Moments later, Jackson could hear the shower running. He grimaced as he stood, stretching his cramped muscles again, before walking to the phone to call Richard, who was no doubt working himself up into a state.

He had no idea what Richard's mobile number was as it was preprogrammed into his own phone. He flicked through the phone book, quickly locating the hotel's number. What was his schedule this morning? He wasn't quite sure but he *was* certain he was supposed to be somewhere in nine minutes' time! Most of his mornings started at eight.

When the hotel operator answered his call, he asked for Richard's room and waited, not liking what was about to happen. 'Richard,' he said into the receiver when the phone was picked up. A split second later he held the phone away from his ear as Richard's voice boomed through. 'Calm down,' he tried. It didn't work. He heard the shower stop and realised that Susie was going to be leaving her house very, very soon. As he'd come in a taxi last night, he had no way of getting back to his hotel—well, no way that wouldn't take another half-hour or more. She'd have to give him a lift.

'Richard,' he said finally, 'you're wasting time. What's my schedule?' He listened intently, his mind working in overdrive. 'All right. Bring me a change of clothes and a clean suit. I'll meet you in the theatre block.' He could at least have a shower and change there. 'Where I am is of little importance now. Just do it, please.' With that, he replaced the receiver. Heading through to the kitchen, his stomach grumbled and he checked the contents of her fridge.

A few minutes later Susie came rushing into the kitchen while he finished his orange juice and bit into an apple. 'Can I get you anything?' he asked.

'Yes. Get out of my house!'

'Not a problem. Which way is the garage?'

'*What?*' Susie exploded. 'You can't come to work with me.'

'Why not? I need to go to the hospital. You're going there. What's the problem?'

She looked at him as though he'd grown an extra head. 'The problem, Professor, is that everyone will see you coming to work in my car, and as you're dressed in casual clothes, they'll put two and two together and make four!'

'So?'

Susie threw her hands up in exasperation. 'Typical of you. You'll be gone tomorrow and I'll have to live with the rumours and gossip—

again.' She didn't have time for this. She reached into the fridge and pulled out a banana before storming out the kitchen, Jackson hard on her heels.

'What do you mean, again? Have we been gossiped about before?'

'Not you and me but me and Walter. Me and Greg. You guys leave and I'm the one who stays.' She headed through the laundry to the outside door.

'Don't lump me in with those two morons. This is different and you know it. Nothing happened last night.'

'You know that and I know that, but the fact remains that we'll be seen arriving together and you'll be leaving tomorrow.'

'What am I supposed to do?'

'Call a taxi and wait.'

'I can't. I'm lecturing at eight.'

'Then you're going to be late no matter what you do.' She locked her house and headed to the garage. She spun on her heel to face him. 'Look, Jackson, I've spent the past six months picking up the pieces of my life since Greg left. People still give me little pitying looks and there are only so many that I can ignore.'

'Susie, you're overreacting. Besides, what does it matter what people say about you? Surely you're above all that.'

Susie was filled with temper and frustration and at his comment she wanted to throw something at him. 'You just don't get it, do you? I don't care what people *think*. They respect me as a surgeon and a professional but this has been going on for far too long and I'm sick of it. There's only so much a girl can take, Jackson, and right at the moment I don't choose to take any more.'

She'd unlocked the garage and the car, noticing that Jackson was determined to get in. He sat beside her as she revved the engine and reversed, pressing the remote control for the garage door to close.

'Drop me a block before the hospital and I'll walk the rest of the way,' he told her quietly, and she started to feel silly for her tirade.

She glanced across at him. 'Listen, I'm sor—'

'No.' He held up his hand. 'It's fine. You don't need to apologise.'

Although his words sounded sincere, the strained silence that followed made Susie realise that things had just changed—again. She shook her head as she pulled to the kerb a block away from the hospital. His smile was forced when he climbed out and started walking. This week had been mixed with exhaustion and exhilaration, and as she watched him walk away she felt a sense of loss.

'What is wrong with you?' she murmured as she pulled back into traffic. It wasn't until she'd reached her designated car park and switched off the engine that the truth hit her. It had been staring her in the face for quite some time but she'd been pushing it away, refusing to admit it.

'I'm in love with him!'

CHAPTER TEN

ON LEGS that felt like lead, Susie walked to her office. How had it happened? *When* had it happened? She shivered from the knowledge as she slumped into her chair, staring out into space.

She was in love with Jackson. Oh, not the way she'd thought she'd been in love with Walter or Greg. This…this was the *real* thing. With the others she'd felt secure, cared for, but with Jackson…she wanted and needed him just as she needed oxygen to breathe. He had become a part of her, a vital, desperate part and one she couldn't bear to be without—yet she had to.

Her door opened and she sprang up from her chair in fright. 'Todd! Don't do that!'

'Do what?' he asked. 'I did knock.' He closed the door behind him. 'Are you all right?'

'Yes. Of course I am,' she replied quickly. 'Why? Don't I look all right?' She smoothed her hands over her trousers. 'What's wrong with the way I look?'

'Nothing,' he said carefully, and placed a file on her desk. 'Spill the beans, Susie.'

'What?'

'Your eyes, your body language...'

'What's wrong with my eyes?' she challenged him, knowing she was behaving like a caged dingo.

'They're wild, filled with disbelief.'

'Oh, no,' she groaned, slumping into her chair and resting her head on the desk.

'What's the problem, Susie?' Todd's tone was concerned.

She knew she could trust him. If there was one thing she would never question Todd over it was his loyalty to her. Slowly she raised her head and looked at him. 'I'm in love with Jackson,' she moaned.

'Yeah. So?'

'What do you mean, *so*?'

'So I've known this since Monday.'

'Monday! No way. I wasn't in love with him on Monday.'

'Ah...but you were well on your way. You should go for it.'

'So you've said.'

'I'll have you know...' Todd waggled his index finger at her '...that my advice is generally spot on.'

'Thank you, my own personal agony aunt, but I don't need any advice. There's nothing to give advice on.'

'But you're in love with him.'

'I know. I was in love with Walter and Greg. I got over them so I shall just get over Jackson, too.'

Todd frowned at her before saying quietly, 'You think so?'

Susie took a deep, cleansing breath and met her secretary's gaze. 'I have to.'

Somehow she managed to pull herself together and concentrate on her work. Theatre with Hilda Kazinksi went extremely well and the success of the operation did much to bolster her failing spirits.

That night she dressed carefully in the last outfit she'd bought for her week as host to the visiting orthopaedic professor. It was his official farewell dinner tonight and she wanted to look perfect. She was desperate to see that spark of desire in his eyes again whilst dreading the thought of seeing him.

Her dress was two-tone, the bodice made from navy velvet and the skirt from pale blue silk. A wide band of navy velvet circled the base of the skirt and Susie had never felt more pretty in a dress than she did in this one. She was glad she'd saved it for last.

She took time with her hair, piling half of it up and leaving the other half to swirl around her shoulders. There was no need for a necklace as the dress had a high neckline. If Jackson planned on nuzzling her neck tonight, he'd just have to think again.

Finally, pleased with her appearance, she drove to the function room where the dinner was being held. Once again, she noted she was seated at Jackson's table and called on every last ounce of determination she had, knowing she would need it to get her through the evening.

The instant she saw him across the crowded room, her stomach began to churn. She propped her elbow up on the bar for support, and as her mouth went dry she reached, with a not-so-steady hand, for her drink.

It was true. It was really true. She hadn't been imagining it after all. She really was in love with Jackson Myers.

He spotted her and, just as she'd known they would, his blue eyes darkened momentarily with repressed desire. He quickly returned his attention to the person talking to him but she could see his impatience in the way he stood, the way he smiled politely and the way his gaze flicked to her another three times in under thirty seconds.

'Wow, boss,' Kyle said as he came up beside her. 'You look dead sexy in that dress.'

'Thank you, Kyle,' she responded, smiling at her registrar as they were called into dinner. 'You look dead handsome in your tux.' He offered her his arm and she took it. She wanted to walk in with Jackson, to talk with him, to listen to him, to soak up everything about him—but at the same time she wanted to keep as far away from him as possible.

It was just too soon. She'd only realised that morning that she was in love with the man and, quite frankly, she needed some time to adjust. Susie wasn't sitting next to Jackson this time, which brought more mixed emotions. She wanted to be next to him, to feel his body close to hers, to breathe in the irresistible scent of him, to fight the pull of his hypnotic gaze, but at the same time she was glad of the reprieve.

Kyle sat on one side of her with Mr Petunia on the other, his wife next to him. Mrs Petunia spoke animatedly of her grandchildren and although Susie smiled and nodded in the right places, she was conscious of every move Jackson made.

Jackson was seated almost directly opposite her and their gazes meshed several times across the large round table. Just after the main course Susie excused herself and headed to the rest-rooms. Once there, she leaned against the wall for support and closed her eyes. He was gorgeous. Gorgeous, sexy and far too close. It pained her that he would leave tomorrow and right now, when she should be making the most of the time they had left together, she was keeping as far away from him as she possibly could.

'Hi, there.'

Susie's eyes snapped open at the other woman's voice and she found herself face to face with one of the theatre nurses. 'Feeling all right?' the nurse asked as she repaired her bright red lipstick.

'Sure,' Susie replied. 'Just a bit tired.'

'I hear the Kazinski hand reconstruction went well.'

'Yes.' Susie nodded quickly. 'Very well.'

The nurse paused and looked over her shoulder before saying, 'I also hear that you and a certain visiting professor have been spending quite a bit of time together.'

Susie didn't need to look in the mirror to know that the colour had just drained from her face. 'Wh-what do you mean?'

'I mean the fact that I saw him get out of your car this morning a block away from the hospital, and I wasn't the only one.' She gave Susie a huge grin. 'So give. What's he like?'

'Like?'

'You know, to kiss? To cuddle? In bed?'

Susie's jaw dropped open in shock. 'That's none of your business.' The instant the words were out of her mouth, she realised she'd incriminated herself totally.

'So you *are* involved. How romantic! Was I right? Is he divorced or is he just…lonely?'

'Oh, this isn't happening,' Susie mumbled as she turned on the cold tap and ran her hands beneath the water. Taking a deep breath and calling on every ounce of professionalism she could muster, she turned off the tap and dried her hands before answering. 'Look, Jackson is a nice man.'

'No kidding.'

'We're *colleagues*. That's all.'

'Yeah, right. I saw him get out of your car at eight o'clock in the morning. I know which hotel he's staying at and you were coming from the opposite direction. I was also at his lecture which started late, and when he finally arrived he was dressed in a suit and his hair was wet as though he'd just had a shower.'

Susie gulped over the hard lump that had formed in her throat. She *hated* being the target of hospital gossip. It had happened twice in the past and she'd vowed that it would never happen again. Losing her temper would do no good, admitting to the rumours would do no good, appealing to the grapevine's sense of compassion would definitely do no good.

She was caught between a rock and a hard place—again—and as usual the guy walked away with no repercussions to face. The nurse before her was waiting for her answer and Susie smiled politely.

'You're a great theatre nurse.'

The other woman frowned. 'As opposed to what?'

'A private eye.' Susie turned on her heel and walked out. Inside, she was shaking like a leaf and thanked her training for making her appear outwardly composed. She tried telling herself she didn't care about the rumours and gossip but it didn't work. She should have made Jackson take a taxi. She should have known that one block from the hospital wouldn't have been sufficient distance for people not to see them together.

'Shoulda, coulda, woulda,' she muttered as she walked over to the now deserted bar and leaned against it. What was she going to do? The pitying glances, the sorrowful looks. They were all going to start again, along with the 'poor Susie' sighs. This time, though, it would hurt more than the others. This time it would tear her heart to shreds. This time she doubted whether she'd ever recover.

Tears started to well in her eyes and she willed them away, massaging her temples, trying desperately to get herself under control. She sniffed and realised she was fighting a losing battle. She bit her lip and closed her eyes, tears falling onto her cheeks which she gently brushed away as she concentrated on some deep breaths.

'Susie?'

Her eyes snapped open, her back went rigid and head turned as she stared wildly at Todd. She relaxed a fraction as he quickly crossed to her side. 'Are you OK?'

His concern was heart-warming but the last thing she needed right now was for Todd to comfort her. She squared her shoulders and nodded. 'I'll be fine. Just don't...touch me or

I'll lose it.' She held up her hand to stop him as she spoke. He nodded in understanding and waited for her to speak. 'One of the nurses just informed me that...' She took a deep breath and exhaled. 'That...um...Jackson and I are being gossiped about.'

'Oh, fair dinkum,' Todd spat. 'Why can't they leave you alone?' He reached out a hand to her but she stepped away, her back bumping into the wall. 'I've been kind of trying to see if there were any rumours all week long but there was nothing. Then again, people probably wouldn't tell me, knowing I'd pass it back to you.'

Susie found she was able to smile at his protectiveness. 'You're a good friend.' She sucked in a big breath, hiccuping a little as she did so, before breathing out. 'Right now, though, I need to pull myself together and—'

'There you are.' Jackson's voice pierced the confidential air around Todd and herself. He crossed to where she was standing in the corner. 'I've been worried.'

Her heart lunged with happiness at his words, making her feel as though everything would turn out right. He'd been worried about her. He'd been conscious of the time she'd been away from the table. Here was the man she loved, being so…so…darn cute. She tore her gaze away from him to glance at Todd. Her secretary's eyes were filled with a question—did she want him to stay? Slowly Susie shook her head and reluctantly Todd stepped away but not before he glared menacingly up at Jackson.

'What was that look for?' Jackson asked, after Todd had left.

'He's as protective as one of my brothers,' she murmured. She crossed her arms in front of her chest. She was on the defensive and she needed to stay firm in her annoyance of the situation.

'Why does he think you need protecting from me? He knows about us?'

'Yes, and so does the rest of the hospital, it seems.'

'What?'

'People saw you getting out of my car this morning.' She shook her head. 'I knew I should have made you take a taxi.'

'So this is all my fault?'

'Yes.'

'How do you figure that?'

'Because you'll be gone tomorrow.'

'So?'

'So I'm the one who's going to be left with the rumours, gossip, pitying looks.'

'And you think you're the only person who's ever been gossiped about in hospitals? I had to endure everything and more when Alison died. She was a secretary there so not only did I get pitying looks and sympathy, left, right and centre, I also had to deal with people avoiding me because they didn't know what to say. For six months, until I left to come away on the professorship, people avoided me. I didn't have normal conversations with my theatre staff except for, ''Pass me that retractor''!' He spoke in a harsh whisper, one that cut through Susie's self-indulgence like a scalpel.

'In some ways it was a relief to leave, to get away from anyone who had anything to do with Alison and my life. To concentrate on work so I could forget the pain I was feeling, the way I was slowly being eaten up inside. To get away from the quiet whispers in the hospital corridors that stopped suddenly every time I walked by. So, Dr Monahan, you are not the only one to have encountered the hospital grapevine.'

Susie nodded once, acknowledging his words. 'But I can't escape,' she said softly. 'This is where I'm employed and although I plan to do research next year, I'll still remain on as a consultant. This is the hospital where I've been gossiped about more than once. It may not have been the magnitude of yours but, still, the words, the looks—they can really hurt and I'm sick of it happening.' Her words were calm as she gazed up at him.

'Susie, I—'

'I'm going home now.'

He gazed at her for a long, drawn-out moment and the whole world seemed to slip away, leaving the two of them the only people on earth. They'd connected. In five long, hectic days they'd made a dramatic connection and one that had left Susie madly in love with the man in front of her.

Jackson nodded and stepped back. 'I'll make your apologies.'

'I'd appreciate it.' Susie forced her legs to work as she walked past him.

'Are we still on for tomorrow?'

Mallory and Nick were expecting them and Susie knew that the more time she spent with Jackson, the harder it would be for her to let go. 'Yes.'

His smile brightened and she felt the full effects of it. 'Sleep sweet, Susie.' As much as he wanted to scoop her up and kiss her senseless, Jackson knew he couldn't. He clamped down on the feeling, knowing it wouldn't do him any good. He'd just have to cool his heels until tomorrow. He watched the way she walked, her head held high, her bag clutched tightly in her hand. Her hips swayed slightly and he felt a tightening in his gut. She was dazzling and she'd dazzled him all week long.

Even as he allowed himself to acknowledge these feelings, hard on their heels came ones of guilt and remorse. He knew he was a free man legally, but emotionally Jackson wasn't sure if he was ready to move on. There was still so much he needed to deal with, so much in Melbourne waiting for him to return to.

If…and it was a *big* if…there was going to be anything permanent between Susie and himself, he owed it to both of them to deal with his past first before moving on to the future. For the present? He raked a hand through his hair. For the present he was going to enjoy her company. The consequences would come later. Of that he had little doubt.

As they'd arranged, Susie picked Jackson up bright and early on Saturday morning, visually devouring him the instant he climbed into her car. He smiled, leaned over and kissed her briefly on the lips. She returned his smile and they started off.

It was as though by unspoken mutual consent both were determined to enjoy their last day together—away from the hospital, away from patients and colleagues, away from prying eyes and away from pagers and phones.

Breakfast was delicious, with Jackson demanding she taste some of his eggs while she insisted he eat a mouthful of her pancakes. She was delighted with the intimacy they created and for a moment allowed herself to believe it was real. That they were really a couple and that they would always want to taste what the other had.

It was the way her parents were, the way her married siblings were, and it was what she wanted for her life. It was the little things in life that made a person happy. The little unique things, the little fun things and the little considerate things.

Today—right at this moment—she was happy. Happier than she'd ever been. The man she loved was beside her, his hand resting possessively on her thigh as she drove. She was still amazed to acknowledge that she loved him. She giggled.

'What are you laughing at?' he asked as she took the turnoff to Appleton.

'Nothing. I'm just… I'm happy.'

His smile melted her insides and the quick squeeze he gave her leg sent spirals of desire shooting throughout her body. She quickly returned her attention to the road, especially as it was now beginning to wind and curve.

Jackson marvelled at the scenery, the large evergreen trees topped with ivy which were so natural, so untouched. He glanced at Susie, the smile still on her face as she concentrated on negotiating the curves and hairpin bends.

Today he felt as though he could breathe, and he was loving it. They'd called a truce, happy and content to be with each other. When she'd told him she was happy, a warmth had spread through him. *He* had made her happy. Being with *him* was making her happy and if he owned the truth, he felt the same way.

He marvelled once again at how different everything was between Susie and himself. The way they'd met, the instant attraction, the desire that neither had been able to control. This was so primal, so necessary. Everything was so different from the ways he'd courted in the past—even with Alison.

Alison. He shook his head and pushed the thought away, ignoring the stab of guilt as he tucked his wife into a far corner of his mind. Today wasn't about Alison. Today wasn't about decisions. Today was about spending time with Susie.

'Here we are,' she announced, bringing him back to reality. She pulled into a driveway and switched off the engine.

They climbed out and walked to the front door. Susie rang the doorbell and looked across at Jackson. He took her hand in his and gave it a squeeze. Moments later the loud thumping sounds of children's shoes on wooden floors could be heard before the door was swung open.

'Susie!' Rebekah squealed as she unlocked the screen door.

'Hello,' Edward chimed in, then looked up at Jackson. 'Who are you?'

'I'm Jackson,' he said. 'A friend of Susie's.'

Nick and Mallory's housekeeper, Arlene, came down the corridor, wiping her hands on her apron as Rebekah led them into the house. 'Hi, Susie. Welcome, Professor Myers.'

'Jackson, please,' he insisted, and offered his hand in greeting.

Arlene frowned. 'I'm afraid Nicholas and Mallory aren't here, Susie, but your arrival couldn't have been more timely.'

'Come and have a look at my cars,' Edward was saying as he tugged on Susie's arm.

'Just a minute, sweetheart,' she said as she scooped him up for a quick cuddle.

'They can't stay,' Rebekah told her three-year-old brother. 'They have to go to the hospital. Remember?'

'Oh.' Edward wriggled down.

'Becka's right.' Arlene turned her attention to the children. 'Why don't you two go and play for now? Go on,' she said, shooing them with her hands. 'I'll be there in a minute.'

Both children reluctantly walked back up the corridor. 'Bye, Susie,' Rebekah said and Edward copied her. 'Come back next weekend.'

'I'll try,' she said, blowing them kisses.

'There's been an emergency,' Arlene said once the children were out of earshot. 'A car accident. A young local woman, Annabel Dexter, and her son, Brayden.' Arlene lowered her voice. 'He's three and a good friend of Eddie's. Apparently she lost control and the car hit a tree.'

'When did it happen?' Jackson asked.

'A while ago now. Mallory and Nick are both on the retrieval team,' she explained to Jackson, 'but Nick was hoping you'd go to the hospital so you're ready for when the patients arrive.'

Susie nodded. 'I know the drill. Thanks, Arlene.' She turned and headed back through the door.

'I'm so sorry your visit has to be cut short.'

'I'm glad we're here to help,' Jackson told her. When they were in the car and on their way to the hospital, Jackson asked, 'Do you often come here to help out?'

'Sure. Several staff do. Our orthopaedic department supports a clinic here and I'm on the rotation. We also help out in emergencies so I know my way around.'

'Good.' He watched her for a second, concern drawing his brows together. 'There's something else bothering you,' he stated.

Susie parked the car outside the hospital and turned to look at him, surprised that he'd picked up on her emotions. 'What makes you say that?'

'Your body is tense and you're frowning in concern.'

'Oh. Well, yes, I am concerned…about Mallory. Years ago she was involved in a terrible accident and says she only survived because of the retrieval team personnel.'

'So now she does retrieval herself.' Jackson nodded.

'Yes, but each time she attends one, she has horrible nightmares. Although, since she married Nick six years ago, she's said they haven't been too bad.'

'We just go on,' he murmured with a shrug. 'We face what we have to face and we deal with it.'

'Yes.' She sighed.

'Come here.' His mouth was warm and comforting when it pressed to hers. Susie closed her eyes, revelling in the bursts of desire that spread through her. The kisses were soft and reassuring, both of them drawing from them extra strength to deal with whatever was about to come their way. 'Ready?' Jackson gazed down into her eyes, holding firmly to his self-control, knowing that if he stared for too long he'd lose himself completely and now certainly wasn't the time.

'Let's go.'

When they entered the hospital, Susie was welcomed like an old friend. Everyone was friendly and professional, just as he'd experienced in every other hospital he'd been in during the past year. The difference here was that he was just a colleague of Susie's. She hadn't introduced him as Professor but merely Jackson Myers. He liked it. He liked the feeling of being incognito, of not being questioned about techniques or differences in methods. Instead, he was allowed to do his job—that of helping out in an emergency.

Fifteen minutes later they received information that both patients were out of the wreck and on their way. A list of injuries were presented and Susie and Jackson discussed how best to deal with them. They notified Brisbane General as well as contacting the children's hospital. The helicopter was ready, the theatre and radiology staff were waiting to go and, as the orthopaedic surgeon in charge, Susie was starting to get impatient for the patients to arrive.

Annabel Dexter's list of injuries was long. Both legs were fractured—the left and right femur as well as the right tibia and fibula. Her right shoulder was dislocated and her right humerus had sustained a break. She had concussion but had regained consciousness during the rescue.

She also had internal injuries, which Nick would be required to stabilise, and as he was heading back in the ambulance with the patient, they'd decided that Jackson and Nick should start on Annabel.

The report on her son, Brayden, wasn't so bad. He'd hit his head so they'd need to check that out, but he didn't appear to be suffering from concussion. His left leg was broken, as was his right arm. The shock the child had endured was what tugged at Susie's heart strings.

She'd almost specialised in paediatric orthopaedics but had found that she hadn't been able to bear the suffering children went through. She had been more of an emotional wreck than the child. She'd get Brayden sorted out and send him off to Brisbane in the helicopter to let the experts take care of him.

When the first ambulance finally arrived, the entire A and E was buzzing with activity.

They had a look at the patient and ordered X-rays, and while the pictures were being taken Nick crossed to Susie's side and hugged her.

'Thanks for being here.'

'Good timing,' she murmured, before introducing Jackson.

The two men shook hands. 'Sorry to be meeting under such circumstances,' Nick said, 'but at least an emergency will be a bit of a change for you.'

Jackson nodded. 'You're not wrong there.'

'The second ambulance should be here any minute now.' Nick was clearly in control. After all, this was his hospital. 'Susie, you'll be checking Brayden out. I presume the chopper's ready to go to Brisbane?'

'Yes,' they answered in unison, and smiled at each other.

'Excellent.'

'Where's Mallory?'

Nick shook his head and raked his hand frustratedly through his hair. 'She was squeezing herself out of the wrecked car when I left.'

'What was she—?' Susie asked, but Nick cut her off.

'Oh, you know Mal. We couldn't get to Brayden so she squeezes herself into the car and manages to pass him out. Only problem was that once Brayden was out, a branch fell onto the car and trapped her.'

Jackson's eyes widened. 'Your wife is trapped in a car?'

'Yeah. Pretty typical stunt of Mallory's,' Nick growled. 'The rest of the crews are there, getting her out.'

'She couldn't wait for them to cut the roof off the car?' Jackson asked, watching the other man's expression closely. Here was a man who loved his wife completely, yet he was still able to let her be herself.

'Well, she will now.'

'I'd be livid if my wife did something like that,' Jackson commented.

Susie felt as though he'd slapped her. She knew it was an idle comment but his wife hadn't been a popular topic of conversation between them during the past week. And, besides, she found his statement to be rather chauvinistic. Was Jackson *really* that dominating?

'I *am* livid,' Nick replied. 'But I also accept that Mallory has a life of her own—and a will as strong as iron, I might add. Although on this occasion I have to say that I agreed with her. Brayden was becoming far too distressed with the situation. We couldn't wait for the emergency crew with the jaws of life to arrive to cut the poor kid out. We know Brayden. He comes to our house to play and I could just see Mallory thinking what if Edward had been in the car?'

'First lot of X-rays are coming out of the processor,' the radiologist informed them.

'Thanks. Jackson, come and take a look with me. Susie, you stay and wait for Brayden.' Nick checked his watch. 'I expected him to be here by now.'

'Sure.' She watched the two of them go, mulling over what she'd learned. Was Jackson a domineering man? Would a woman lose herself if she were with him? Had Alison? Perhaps Alison had been the type of woman who'd wanted a dominant husband. Someone who would make decisions for her and protect her.

Certainly there was nothing wrong with that but Susie had learnt what she *needed* from a long-term relationship the hard way. Twice she had almost lost herself. First with Walter and then with Greg. Both men had wanted her to change, to fit in with *their* plans, not willing to support her in what *she* wanted to do.

Surely Jackson wasn't the same? Oh, he'd been domineering with his staff but that was different. She herself had put her foot down once or twice. Generally, though, she was a peace-maker, but that didn't mean she was going to be walked all over—again!

His words repeated themselves in her mind. 'I'd be livid if my wife did something like that.' Did he still think of Alison as his wife?

Of course he did. She'd only died eighteen months ago and for some people falling in love once was all they wanted. Was Jackson like that?

Her head was starting to hurt and she knew she had to focus. Brayden would be arriving any minute now and she wouldn't do him, or his mother, any good if she was stuck in her daydreams about Jackson.

As the ambulance sirens could be heard drawing near, Susie forced all thoughts of Jackson to the back of her mind. She was a professional and many times throughout her career she'd had to switch off what she called her 'personal brain' and switch on the 'doctor brain'. This time, though, it was a lot harder to do and she knew why. Although she'd thought herself in love with both Walter and Greg, her feelings then had been nothing compared to what she felt now. So why did she have so many unanswered questions? If she really loved Jackson, shouldn't she be able to trust him, too?

CHAPTER ELEVEN

AN HOUR later, Susie was satisfied with Brayden's condition. It was nowhere near as bad as she'd anticipated. Under a general anaesthetic she'd managed to manipulate and re-align the bones, thankful that both his fractures were non-compound, therefore only requiring plaster casts.

He was bruised quite badly, especially across his abdomen where his safety-harness had restrained him, but she could find no other injuries and had left him sleeping off the effects of the general anaesthetic in Recovery.

She'd decided not to transfer him at this stage and requested the nursing staff to notify the children's hospital in Brisbane. When she'd come out of Theatre, the Dexter family was waiting for news of Brayden. Susie was eager to assist Jackson with Annabel's surgery but it wasn't professional to ignore them.

She spent ten minutes giving them a run-down of the injuries before excusing herself and heading to Theatre. When she arrived, Nick had finished repairing Annabel's internal rupture of her large intestine, as well as her bladder.

'Good timing, Susie,' he said from behind his mask. 'I'll leave you and Jackson to continue. Has Mallory returned yet?'

'Not yet,' she replied, keeping her tone neutral. She had been getting a little worried, too. 'I'll go check.'

'Let us know when she arrives,' Susie called over her shoulder as Nick left the room. She looked at Jackson over the top of her mask. 'Femurs?'

'I've stabilised the bleeding but the fractures still need open reduction and internal fixation.'

'How about you lead on the lower limb injuries and I'll lead on the upper?' she suggested, and saw the twinkle in his eyes. Her heart lurched but she forced it under control. She wasn't in Theatre to flirt with him, she was here to work.

'Sounds like a plan,' he responded, and they concentrated on debriding the wound before fixing the comminuted fracture back together. They worked together in a companionable silence for the next few hours, both giving clear instructions to staff they weren't used to working with.

There was no fracture of the shoulder so Susie was able to relocate the neck of humerus into place. The humerus was a comminuted fracture which required Susie to piece together the bony fragments with plates and interfragmentary screws.

'It's a pleasure to watch you work, Dr Monahan,' Jackson commented as she closed the wound in layers.

'Why, thank you,' she replied, her eyes gleaming over the top of her mask. When they were both satisfied with Annabel's condition, they finished off and handed her over to the care of the nursing staff.

'Still no word about Mallory,' Susie mused as she degowned. She checked the clock. They'd been in Theatre for quite some time— almost three and a half hours. 'Surely Nick would have called through.'

'Perhaps they've been caught up with the family,' Jackson reasoned. 'After all, they are close friends.'

'Susie?'

She turned around to see one of the theatre nurses looking at her with a stunned expression. 'What's wrong?' Instinct had always played a big part in Susie's life—especially on the medical side—and right now she knew there was something wrong.

'It's—'

'Mallory,' Susie and the nurse said at the same time. 'What's happened?'

'Triage Sister called and said Mallory's broken her leg. She was trapped in the car, and just as they were about to get her out another branch fell, squashing her leg.'

Susie looked at Jackson, glad to have a lower-limb specialist with her. 'When is she due?'

'Any time now.'

'Thanks.' Susie tossed the word over her shoulder as she and Jackson hot-footed it back to A and E, only to find Nick pacing around anxiously, his eyes filled with anguish and pain. 'Nick.'

He spun around and glared at her with eyes of steel. 'You've got to fix her up, Susie.'

'I'm sure it's not as bad as it seems.'

'Susie, you're on staff here so I'll hand over to you. I'm going to—' He broke off as the ambulance sirens wailed. 'She's here,' he whispered, and rushed out.

Susie turned to Jackson. 'You wanted emergencies—here's your next patient.'

He gave an ironic laugh. 'Half my luck.' He placed his arm about her shoulders and gave a little squeeze. 'Will you be all right assisting me? I mean, she is your friend.'

Susie took a deep breath and sighed. 'I'll be fine.'

'That's what I like to hear.' He squeezed her shoulder again then let go, and Susie experienced a momentary sense of loss. The man only had to brush his fingertips lightly over her skin and she was all but panting for him. She shook her head, clearing her thoughts as the barouche was wheeled in. Nick was by his wife's side, firmly holding her hand.

'Hey, Mallory.' Susie smiled at her friend. 'Nice to see you again.'

Mallory chuckled and then groaned. 'Ow.'

'What's wrong, honey?'

Jackson noted that Nick was no longer a doctor but an anxious husband. It was clear his wife meant everything to him. Had he behaved in a similar way when he'd arrived at the hospital after Alison's accident? No. He'd been calm and in control. It had only been later, much later, that the numbness had started to set in.

'Nice to meet you, Mallory,' Jackson said. 'Let's get her into an examination cubicle so we can take a better look at that leg.' Jackson stepped aside, waiting for the barouche to be wheeled through before following. Susie placed a hand on his arm.

'Go easy on Nick,' she said compassionately, and he nodded. Mallory's pain relief was under control and, after having a good look at the wound site, Jackson wrote up the X-ray request form.

'Let's get some pictures of your leg and get you into Theatre.'

'Does she need a CT scan?' Nick asked anxiously.

'Nick!' It was Mallory who spoke her husband's name. 'Just relax. I couldn't be with a finer surgeon if I'd planned this.' Her voice was soft and she tugged her husband's arm, urging him closer. Susie watched as Mallory kissed her husband. She sighed and looked away, not wanting to meet Jackson's gaze. This was what she wanted—so desperately—and she wanted it with Jackson.

'Off to Radiology,' Jackson said into the silence that followed, and Mallory was wheeled away with Nick still glued to her side. He glanced across at Susie, only to find her studying the floor. He could feel the atmosphere between them—one filled with the unspoken words of their hearts. In that instant he acknowledged that Susie was more dear to him than Alison had been and the thought terrified him.

She cleared her throat. 'I think I'll…um…get a cup of tea.' Without looking at him, she headed out of the cubicle. Jackson stared at the wall, trying desperately to come to terms with the revelation. How could he possibly feel more for Susie than he had for Alison? He'd loved Alison. She'd been his wife.

This wasn't right. It couldn't be.

'Doctor?' One of the nurses cut through his thoughts. 'Is there anything you need?'

Susie. He needed Susie! 'Ah…no. Thank you. I'm just thinking things through.' He stalked out of the cubicle and headed towards the tearoom, his steps growing hesitant and slow as he neared it. If he needed Susie, if he felt so strongly about her, then that would mean he was in love with her.

He stopped short. No. He had to be wrong, but everything he felt, every time he thought about Susie, about her being in an accident like Mallory's or worse—like Alison's—his heart felt as though it was being torn in half.

He turned on his heel and headed to Radiology. Now wasn't the time to think about this. Now wasn't the time to analyse. He had surgery to perform and he welcomed the distraction with enthusiasm.

Susie concentrated on the road, switching on her headlights as dusk crept over them. They were almost there—almost at the end. She indicated for the airport turnoff, hoping that Jackson would say something and soon.

During the hour-long drive they'd spoken hardly a word. Had she done something wrong or was he merely exhausted? After all, this was supposed to be his day off and he'd spent most of it in Theatre.

She'd marvelled at his skill once more as he'd reduced Mallory's comminuted fracture of the femur. A CT scan had been necessary to show up the shattered bony fragments, and slowly but surely he'd pieced the bone back together. Her friend was now recovering without complications in Appleton General Hospital, her doting husband now annoying the nursing staff.

Jackson rested his head back and closed his eyes, absorbing the strains of Mozart that filled the car. He knew he had to say something to

Susie. All too soon he'd be getting on a plane and heading for his next destination. Richard had been annoyed that he hadn't made it back in time but had reluctantly agreed to pack his things and meet him at the airport.

Feelings of guilt had swamped him completely once he'd realised he was in love with Susie. In one short week he'd met and fallen in love with another woman! He'd never thought it possible, especially as his love for Alison had grown slowly but steadily over the course of many months.

But this was a different kind of love. Alison was gone. He would always love her, but he had to move on. And what he felt for Susie was deep, soul-filled and heart-wrenching.

His feelings of desire for Susie were incredibly strong. He couldn't control them and the need to have Susie with him had only increased with every passing minute.

She pulled into the airport car park and eased the car into a vacant spot. Without turning off the engine, she turned to face him, her lips tight and thin. 'Thanks for everything today, especially for operating on Mallory.'

Jackson realised she was hoping to kick him out and keep on going, but he had other plans. Leaning over, his hand brushed against the inside of her leg. Ignoring her gasp of surprised desire, he turned the ignition key, silencing the engine. 'Walk me in.' He climbed from the car, striding around to open her door.

'I don't want to.' She stayed where she was.

He took the key out of the ignition, noticing she made no effort to stop him. 'Please.'

Susie gazed into his eyes, her stomach churning with butterflies while tears welled in her eyes and her lower lip started to tremble. 'I can't.' The words were forced out.

He reached down and took her hands in his, urging her carefully. 'Please,' he repeated. Jackson was aware that she was angry with him and he accepted it. Both were caught up on an emotional roller-coaster.

'Why? You haven't spoken a word to me for the past hour.' She wrenched her keys back off him and locked the Jaguar.

'Sorry. I've had a lot on my mind.' Jackson caught her arm as she started to walk off, tugging her closer. Clamping his arms firmly about her, he held her against his body as he leant back against the car. 'Susie.'

Her name was a caress as his mouth met hers in a hungry, fiery and consuming kiss. He never wanted it to end. He wanted to take her with him, for her to be with him for ever. She had to come. She had to see that he couldn't go on without her. Rational thought seemed far away as he intensified the kiss.

Susie moaned in delight, giving everything she had to him. She wanted him to stay. She wanted to stop him from getting on the plane. The plane was her enemy. It would take him away, away from her—and she couldn't bear it.

'Don't go!'

'Come with me!'

The words were torn from both of them the instant they broke apart. Jackson gazed down at her. He knew she felt an overpowering attraction but he wondered just how deep it went. 'Come with me,' he repeated, and watched as the glossy desire disappeared from her eyes, to be replaced by one of confusion.

'On the tour?' Her breath was still coming out in gasps as she struggled for control. He wanted her to go with him and it was the sweetest thing a man had ever said to her. She also knew it was ridiculous. *He* knew it was ridiculous. She smiled at him as what he'd said started to penetrate her mind. He didn't want to leave her and her heart sang with the knowledge.

'I don't mean the tour—I mean to Melbourne.'

'Melbourne?' She frowned.

'Move to Melbourne, Susie. Be with me.'

'Melbourne!' She forced a laugh. But as she gazed at him she realised he was serious. 'You really want me to move to Melbourne?'

'Why not? I could get you a job at my hospital or another hospital if you didn't want to work in the same place. What we have… together…Susie, it's…special.'

'Special enough for me to give up my work, my house, my family, my…*my* life?' She stared at him incredulously. 'I have a research grant to complete. I have patients. I can't just up and move to Melbourne simply because you want me to. Why don't you move to Brisbane? Take on the job as head of department! Why should *I* be the one to change?'

She moved against his arms and he reluctantly let her go.

'What is it with the men in my life?' she asked rhetorically.

'What?' Jackson crossed his arms defensively over his chest and Susie tried desperately hard not to focus on the way his muscles rippled beneath his shirt.

'Did Alison always go along with whatever you wanted?'

'Yes, but I don't see what—'

'I thought so.'

'What does that mean?'

'Jackson!' Richard's voice pierced the air. He was rushing towards them, his face creased with agitation and worry. 'I didn't think you were going to make it. They've just called our flight for the second time. Most of the passengers are on board.' As he drew closer, Susie watched the surprise flicker across his face. 'Susie! Come to see Jackson off, eh? Well, that's very good of you but we *have* to go.'

Susie looked back at Jackson, at that strong jaw of his clamped firmly together, his eyes blazing with anger. This wasn't how she'd envisioned their parting.

'I'm coming,' Jackson growled and without another word he turned and started to walk away. Tears welled in her eyes and spilled over as she watched him go. This wasn't how it was supposed to be.

'Damn it!' Jackson muttered before turning again and striding back, hauling her into his arms and pressing his lips to hers in a punishing kiss. Fire, anger and rage burned through

him and into her as his mouth moved possessively and firmly over hers.

In the next instant he'd let her go and
stalked away, this time not looking back. Susie
glanced quickly at Richard's expression of disbelief. He looked at her and then his boss, then
back to her again. He nodded as though the
past few days were starting to make sense.

Susie couldn't take it any more. Spinning
around, she fumbled with her keys, trying desperately to get the right key into the lock, but
her hand wouldn't stop shaking. Her vision
blurred and she brushed away the tears impatiently.

Sniffing, she looked up to where Jackson
had last been—only to find that both he and
Richard had disappeared inside the building,
swallowed from her view.

Finally she managed to get the right key in
and unlocked the door before slumping behind
the wheel. She rested her head forward as the
sobs began to rack her body. Anger, frustration
and desolation settled over her like a blanket
of fog.

She'd fought the attraction between them
and lost. She'd given her heart and lost but
she'd vowed long ago never to sacrifice her

independence for a man. At least there she had won...or had she?

'Two days,' she grumbled as she stopped at a red light. 'Ten weeks and two days. The pig.' Impatiently Susie drummed her hands on the wheel as she tried not to think about every one of the last seventy-one days, and here she was, driving to work on a Monday morning, embarking on day number seventy-two.

The light turned green and she thankfully continued on her way. She needed to be moving. She needed her mind to be occupied at all times because when it wasn't, Jackson was all she could think about. And she didn't want to think about him. 'The pig,' she muttered again as she indicated to turn into the doctors' car park.

'What the—' She stopped and stared at the car parked in her spot. A Jaguar Mark-V. A lightning bolt struck her heart as she manoeuvred her car into another space. Jackson drove a Mark-V.

'Get out of my head,' she growled as she switched off the engine. 'Work, Monahan. All you need to do is focus on work.' Even as she said the words, Susie knew she was kidding herself. She'd been kidding herself for the past ten weeks and two days since Jackson had left. Nothing. She'd heard nothing from him since he'd turned and walked away at the airport.

She climbed from the car, locked it and headed to the department. Christmas had been a shambles, so much so that she'd rostered herself on for New Year, not able to bear spending it alone. Now she was returning after spending a week's holiday with her parents, and she was exhausted.

Her mother had pried every last detail out of her and they'd spent hours dissecting and discussing everything that had happened during Jackson's week-long visit. In some ways Susie had needed the post-mortem as well as her mother's advice. She hadn't *liked* her mother's advice but she'd needed to hear it all the same.

'And what if you were to move to Melbourne?' her mother had asked.

'How can I do that? I'd be sacrificing everything I've worked so hard for. He shouldn't expect me to change my life completely just because I'm in love with him.'

'Is that what he asked?'

'He asked me to move to Melbourne.'

'That's only geography, darling. He didn't ask you to change who you are inside. He didn't ask you not to work, not to have a career. No, Jackson sounds very different from Walter and Greg. He's not asking you to sacrifice your independence but to enhance your life by being with him.'

'What about his wife?'

'People who love and lose are more likely to love again,' her mother said sagely.

'He never said he loved me.'

'And you? Did you tell him how you feel?'

Susie wasn't able to answer. Her eyes filled with tears, her throat choked up and her mouth went dry. Her mother embraced her and held her while she sobbed.

Taking a deep breath, Susie shoved the thoughts aside as she walked up the corridor towards her office. She didn't meet anyone's gaze, knowing she'd see the pitying looks or the sympathetic smiles that were still floating around thanks to the rumours about her and Jackson's split. This time, though, the gossip had affected her worse than before, probably because this time she had really been in love. Her office door was open so she walked right in but stopped short in the middle of the room.

Someone had changed her room around. Her desk, which had been to one side of the room, was now in the centre. The filing cabinets had been shifted. She stared at the paintings on the walls. Even *they* were different.

'Todd!' she yelled, and turned to face the open door. It was then that she noticed her name-plate was missing. 'Todd!' she yelled louder, as the feeling of uncertainty which had started out as a small prickle along her spine gradually consumed her.

Her secretary appeared at the door. 'You bellowed?' he asked as he waltzed in, carrying a file over to the desk. She watched him closely.

'What's going on here?'

He shrugged. 'Just a few changes.'

'Like what?' She scanned the room again.

'Like you're off the hook.'

She turned back to face him, a frown creasing her forehead. 'What hook? What are you talking about?'

'The hospital has appointed a new head of department. You're off the hook.'

'What? When?'

'Last week. The new head came in on Thursday last week to informally introduce himself to the staff, but his first official day is today.'

'I thought I was supposed to be on the panel for the selection committee.'

'You were, but apparently the hospital received an offer too good to refuse.'

'This doesn't make sense,' she sighed, and closed her eyes as she fought the headache that was beginning to take hold. 'What am I supposed to do?'

'Well, I'm sure the new head will explain that to you.'

'When?'

Todd glanced at his watch. 'You have a meeting with him in…six seconds. No, make that five, four, three, two, one—'

'Good morning, Susie.' Jackson watched as she turned in disbelief to look at him. The bags she was holding dropped to the floor. Her blue eyes were wide with shock, her mouth was hanging open and her hands were limp and lifeless by her side. He thought she'd never looked better.

'Will there be anything else, *boss*?' Todd asked, looking directly at Jackson. He walked past Susie to the open door. 'No?' Todd answered his own question. 'Well, then I'll leave you to explain to Dr Monahan what her new role will be in the department.'

'Alone at last,' Jackson said after Todd had closed the door. 'Would you like to sit down, Dr Monahan, and we can begin?'

Susie couldn't move. She could only stare. She followed his movements as he went around the desk and sunk into her chair—*his* chair, she corrected herself. Emotion after emotion swamped her and she struggled to fight for one to cling to.

The first was shock, then surprise and then elation. He was here!

Hard on their heels came annoyance, then anger and then fury. How dared he?

Her eyes narrowed and she slowly closed her mouth and planted her hands firmly on her hips. She raised her chin in defiance at the smile on his lips, which quickly disappeared. She watched him carefully as he eased back in the chair.

'Don't want to sit? Fine, then. As of today, your official position in the department will be Head of Upper Limb. You'll be required to complete one operating session, two clinics and one on-call roster every week, as well as remaining on the rotational roster for Appleton.' He picked up the file Todd had placed on his desk and took out some papers. 'Your salary details are in here, as are the instructions for when departmental and hospital meetings are scheduled.'

'Stop it!' she demanded.

'You don't want the job?' Jackson raised his eyebrows in mock surprise. 'It will give you all the time you need to complete your research, as well as making available to you any patients who might present to A and E and be worthy of your study.'

'You know what I mean. What are you doing here?'

'I'm trying to do my new job.'

'Jackson!'

'All right.' He chuckled and she almost capitulated as the rich sound she'd thought she'd never hear again washed over her. Resolutely she held firmly to her fury and clenched her teeth.

'What are you doing here?'

'Well, it was your idea in the first place.'

'What?'

He shrugged. 'I took your advice and applied for the job. The hospital knew my credentials and hired me. Effective immediately.'

'Why?' It was hard to get the word out of her mouth but Susie managed. It was a question she desperately needed answered. Why was he here? Why had he come back?

He stood and slowly walked towards her. 'Do you really need to ask?' The look in his eyes told her what she wanted to know but she also needed to hear the words. She didn't want there to be any mistakes this time.

He was getting closer and she wasn't quite ready for him yet. She held up a hand to stop him. Thankfully, he acceded. 'Two and a half months!'

'I know.'

'Ten weeks and two days.'

He nodded. 'I know.'

'Seventy-one sleepless nights, endless days and now…now you just waltz in here and take over my job?'

'A job you didn't want,' he reminded her.

'That's not the point!' she yelled. Her lower lip began to tremble and she fought to control the rising bubble of hysteria that threatened to engulf her.

'What *is* the point?'

'How could you do this to me? How could you just leave me like you did? This is day number seventy-two! Seventy-two!' she repeated, and he nodded. 'That's over one thousand seven hundred hours!'

He checked his watch. 'One thousand, seven hundred and eighteen hours and twelve minutes. All of them unbearable.'

Susie's lips parted as the pent up air escaped her lungs. Her eyes misted over with tears and she sniffed.

'Don't,' he groaned, and covered the remaining distance between them. Susie put out her hands to stop him but this time he ignored them, crushing her to him. 'Don't cry, my sweet Susie.' His mouth was warm and possessive on hers.

'Susie,' he groaned again, and folded his arms about her. 'It's over. It's over.'

Susie clung to him, desperate to believe his words. 'I love you,' she sobbed into his shoulder. She eased her head back to look into his eyes, her lips quivering. 'I love you,' she repeated. 'Don't leave me again.'

'Shh.' Jackson brought his mouth to hers once more, silencing her. 'I won't,' he promised. 'Never.' He held her for a good five minutes, marvelling at how incredible she felt. Susie loved him. She loved him! 'I took this job,' he said, softly stroking her hair, 'because I was determined we should be together. I was determined to move to Brisbane, to work with you every day, to court you, to do it right.

'When I went back to Melbourne...' he paused '...things were...different. Not at all how I remembered. The house Alison and I lived in felt as though it belonged to someone else. I realised then that I wasn't the same any more. I'd changed. I was a different person inside. There are still some issues I need to work through…but I can't do it alone. I need you to help me, Susie.'

He edged her back and tilted her chin up so their gazes could meet. 'I loved Alison. It was a love that grew slowly and steadily over time and I was…content. When she died, a part of me died right along with her, and I thought it would be impossible to go on.'

Susie's heart lurched at his words and she brought her hand up to caress his cheek. He turned and kissed her hand.

'Yet when I left you at the airport to continue with my tour, the pain, the separation from you was sheer torture. But I still felt guilty about Alison, and it took me quite some time to come to terms with everything.'

'Jackson, you don't—'

He placed a finger over her lips. 'Let me finish. Susie, I know that I can finally move on, and I want to be with you. I love you. More than anything in the world.'

Fresh tears welled in her eyes but these were tears she didn't mind. Tears of happiness.

'With you, I'm not just content—I'm extremely satisfied. I'm not just happy—I'm ecstatic. I'm not just in love—I'm devoted. With passion, with adoration, with tenderness.' He kissed away the tears that trickled down her cheeks. 'I need you, Susie.' He pressed a soft and persuasive kiss on her lips. 'Be my wife.'

She gasped at his words, dazed by what had taken place.

'Let me show you I'm not like those other jerks who broke your heart. I don't want to ruin your independence, I want to embrace it, meld it with my own. I love your intellect, the way we can talk about operating techniques, to share the highs and the lows of our jobs. I've never had that with anyone before, but when I found it with you it was as though a part of me became complete. Then another part and then another. Be my wife,' he urged. 'Complete me.'

His mouth was once more hungry and possessive as it met hers in a kiss filled with passion and promise. The promise of a long and devoted life together.

'Say yes,' he ground out as he nibbled his way to her ear lobe. 'Say yes.'

'I will.' She laughed, happier than she'd ever been in her life. 'If you'd give me half a chance.' Goose-bumps shivered down her body as he continued his assault. Giggling, she planted her hand in his hair and gently tugged his head away. 'Jackson!'

'Sorry. It's been seventy-two days, remember.'

'Forget them.' Her words were filled with love, love for the man who was her soul-mate, her other half. 'I'll agree to complete you if you complete me. Jackson, you don't need to show or prove anything to me—because you've already done it. I'm not talking about moving to Brisbane but the fact that you accept me just as I am. No man has ever done that before. You're the first—and the last.' She brushed her lips across his. 'Marry me quickly.'

'As you wish.' His mouth met hers in a mutual declaration of love, one they were both willing to contribute to and work at. 'How am I going to be able to keep my hands off you?' he groaned as he buried his face in her neck, unable to resist kissing the soft skin. 'Working with you every day. Sitting next to you in departmental meetings. I don't know if my self-control can take it.'

'Or my patellar reflexes.' She laughed.

Jackson raised his head to look at the woman he loved. The woman who had made him the happiest man on the face of the earth. He smiled at her.

'I guess we'd better work out some…' she paused and raised her eyebrows suggestively '…guidelines, then.'

His gaze darkened with desire. 'I look forward to it, Dr Monahan.'

'So do I, Professor!'